Beneath Stone and Sacrifice

Melissa Wright

BENEATH STONE AND SACRIFICE

Nim had stolen a lot of things in her time working for the Trust but never a throne. She stared at the silver crown on the desk before her, unease dancing through her gut. Nimona Weston had been born to court then cast out for her family's ties to magic, bound by a tether so dark that she could barely speak of it. She was about to become a queen.

"Fates take us." It was not precisely a helpful thing to say, but she had nothing else. Her contract with the Trust had been broken, but Nim was hardly free. The footing they held was too treacherous to allow her to even draw an easy breath.

Warrick, sitting across from her in the dim light of his private study, said nothing. Her lone savior, he'd been outed not only as heir to Inara but as a man who held magic in his blood. As a traitor to the kingdom.

It had not stopped him from taking the throne. Nim's memory of that moment was still fresh—Warrick in the center of the throne room, his magic roiling around him and rumbling through Nim's very bones as the courtiers surrounding them fell. It had been the worst sort of betrayal to the kingdom, never mind that taking power had not been his wish at all.

He watched her now, emotions held in check, a few dark

hairs damp against his temple, where he'd splashed away the remaining evidence of blood. Hours before, Warrick's mother, head of the Trust and enemy of the kingdom, had killed King Stewart.

It had been revealed the king had sired a second heir. Rhen was Warrick's full-blood brother, unlike Calum, who only shared a mother with Warrick. Rhen was the son of the dead king.

Hours before, Warrick had become Nim's husband. Her head was still spinning with the lot of it. No part of her was certain how they were meant to move forward, how to deal with subjects who did not trust their king in a kingdom at the brink of a war, or how to even keep their own fool heads attached to their necks when so many wanted them on the block for their crimes.

She'd no idea what to do or what was next. If there was anything she was sure of, it was that Warrick owed her answers. She glanced up at him in his place across the desk, the crown between them a symbol of all that had gone wrong.

"If you wear it, you become a target." His words were not a threat or a warning, only a fact. She had chosen to stand with him as his queen before the courtiers and officers of the court as he'd claimed Stewart's throne. They wanted him dead, and they would take his queen with him. An intimation—the strange sense of thoughts and emotions that Nim could detect from those who used magic—came from Warrick that she was fairly certain he had meant to hide: if she hadn't taken his hand, if she hadn't stood with him, she might have had a chance to be safe. He wanted nothing more than to protect her, but that chance was gone.

"I was already a target," she said. "If not to Inara, then to the Trust. There's no escaping for me." Her father's bargain had tied her to the magic—a bargain that said Nim was to decide the fate of the heir of Inara. It was no accident the head of the Trust's terms had been so vague. The woman had plans that did not bode well for anyone in the kingdom, particularly her middle son, whom she'd just forced into stealing a throne.

Warrick shook his head, glancing solemnly at the crown. "Seems simple enough, does it not? You have no magic in your blood. They could support your rule."

She barked a laugh. Nim was no queen, no matter that she'd somehow married a not-entirely-usurper king. She'd known royalty and understood a great many things about how the kingdom worked, but that meant nothing. She'd been turned away from good society as a girl. Power was how a person was perceived. Even associating with those who dealt in magic was punishable by hanging.

What Nim and Warrick had done was impossible to imagine. She was bound to magic. He held it in his blood. His becoming king was worse than anything the citizens of Inara could have ever feared, even if Warrick had only acted to save the kingdom from the very thing they should fear most: the Trust.

"They want nothing of me," Nim said. "Less should they find out the hold that magic has on me."

He stood, turning to face the high arched windows on the far wall of his study. "They don't have to know. What they know of me is enough."

Shame colored his admission, despite that Nim could detect nothing of the sort from his expression or tone. His intimations had been coming more clearly, and she could not help but recall what the head of the Trust had said when they'd been alone in her chambers—how Nim was rooting around in their thoughts, as if it had never been their intentions for her to sense them at all.

Calum had perfected the act of communicating through intimations, carefully controlling what he meant to share and how to hold back so that he might lie to Nim and imagine things that would cause her pain. He'd had years of practice at it, since he'd first encountered her as a girl. His talent was what she had come to expect from them. Yet Warrick seemed to let slip emotions he'd no intention of revealing. And Rhen could project his thoughts so effectively that his seemed to tangle with her own. Worse, he had somehow found a way to keep the sense of his magic from her the same way the queen had, so Nim was not aware they were near until it was too late to run.

Outside the window, the sun had risen, never mind that Warrick and Nim had not slept at all. Fates what they were, the pair had spent their wedding night overthrowing a kingdom. It was only what she should have come to expect, she supposed.

Shouts echoed through the corridor, a reminder that their positions were far from settled. Warrick turned from the window, moving around back of Nim to place a hand on her shoulder. He gave it a light squeeze. "We should prepare."

He crossed the room to don the accoutrements of his new station, and she stared after, unsure if he'd managed any reassurance with the touch at all. Rather than confidence and conviction, she felt his concern and uncertainty—and with it the undeniable pull of his magic and the sense that they were about to do something that could never be undone.

She felt as if the warmth had seeped from her, and Nim finally stood, taking the crown from the desk to place it carefully upon her head. It was silver and gemstone, formed into spikes reminiscent of the dagger strapped to her thigh. She sighed, thinking of the crowd of courtiers about to confront her, and wondered whether placing her weapon on the outside of her gown might be more fitting. Deciding a bolder show of power than a mere dagger was called for, she crossed into Warrick's bedchamber—it was unlikely to ever be hers, given the pair would move to an entirely different suite as king and queen—and shook off the complicated thoughts as she headed for the wardrobe that held Wesley's family sword. Wes had given her ample permission to use it after he'd discovered that, unlike him, Nim could actually wield a magical blade. And she wasn't foolish enough to think she stood a chance holding her own against trained soldiers with anything less.

The drawer came open soundlessly, revealing the familiar blanket covering the weapon. But when Nim slid the blanket aside, she found more than the magic-forged sword. Breath seized in her chest, she took in the cane that Calum had carried for all the years he'd been her keeper. Magic throbbed within the carved wood and etched metal, a horrible pulse that made her want to snatch her hand away while somehow drawing her in. She did not touch it. She only stared.

Something moved behind her, and she tossed the blanket back over the weapons. Warrick's breath brushed against the skin of her neck, easing her sudden fear. "I took possession of it when Calum was imprisoned in the castle dungeon."

That was before Nim had stabbed a Trust heir and broken the contract that had held him there. Before Warrick had walked into the Trust to save her and broken the terms of his own bargain. Before Calum had gone free.

"Fates save us," she whispered again.

"I could not abide the violence he committed with it. So long as I live, he'll not use the thing to harm you."

Nim understood. The things Calum had done were difficult to look at, even for her. If she could be glad of anything, it was that he no longer possessed the horrible thing.

Warrick turned her to face him, his arms sliding around her waist. "So long as I am alive, he'll not harm you at all."

"You cannot promise that," she said.

His hand rose to her cheek, thumb grazing her skin. "Then I swear it, my love. For nothing would kill me as quickly as losing you to them."

She was nearly overwhelmed at the emotions coming from him. So dark and powerful, they were full of the loss of his father, the grief and anger at what was being forced upon them, and a devotion to her so fierce that it threatened to take her breath away.

His dark gaze trailed to her lips, where she'd bitten down from a long habit of locking away her reactions.

He came forward slowly then pressed a soft kiss to her lips. He stayed until every restraint she'd built had broken, then he drew away, just as slowly, and the intimations went with him. "I'll see you outside."

He strode from the room as if he hadn't just disassembled her joints, and she leaned against the chest of drawers until she regained her strength. They were about to face something terrible, and he had asked that they might do so together. Until the end.

Nim drew a deep breath, turned to flip the blanket aside once more, then snatched the sword before the magic could call her to touch Calum's horrible cane. She was out the door in moments, sword in hand and wardrobe secure, with a solid plan to request Calum's weapon be moved to somewhere other than where she and Warrick would sleep. When she opened the door to the sitting room, it was with more force than she'd intended. The lot of its occupants startled to attention.

Nim walked into the room to find Maris dressed not as a simple lady's maid but in the uniform of a queen's protector. Whatever stealth the woman might have aimed for before was gone. Nim was queen, and Maris would strike down anyone who tried to harm her. She gave a swift nod, her hand on the hilt of her own sword. Neither had a chance to speak before Wes moved. Nim tossed the sword onto a chair, fully aware of how much pain proximity to the blade would cause him.

He slammed into her with more vigor and familiarity than was usual in what was clearly meant to be a hug. Her arms wound around him, and after a moment, a breath eased out of his lanky frame. With that breath, it was as if she could feel his devastation, his desperate desire for those he cared for to be out of harm's way.

"I know," she whispered. "I'm sorry." She wasn't certain exactly what for—the death of a king, the loss of the sense of safety that came with a kingdom being shaken to its core, or the fact that each of them faced an uncertain future. The recent events had taken away any chance at all of normalcy for Warrick and, in turn, young Wes. Both Nim and Wesley sighed, then he pulled back, glancing sheepishly at her.

Nim held his gaze. There was no shame in what he was feeling. He and Nim had lost everything in each of their parents' long-ago attempts to save King Stewart and keep Inara safe. The task now fell on Nim's and Warrick's shoulders.

"I'll need you," Nim told Wes. "And I'm grateful to have you all." Her gaze fell to Maris, who had not flinched away from the exchange, then to the other guards in the room. Nim realized with a start the man nearest her was Bramwell, one of Warrick's personal guards and a man she'd knocked from a wagon with the very magic-forged sword she'd just tossed onto the chair. She'd wielded it against the man, who well and truly towered over her, and Nim had entirely prevailed. Apologetically, of course. "I'm glad to see you're well," she told the man.

Bramwell's nod seemed to imply the sentiment was mutual, but he noticeably did not make eye contact with her crown.

Maris stepped forward. "Majesty."

The title sent a cold spike of fear through Nim, though she understood Maris's word was merely a question of whether Nim was ready to face the coming task. She was not ready; she might never be. In fact, she would have been an entirely wooden-headed halfwit to let them go through with it at all.

She gave a sharp nod.

Maris's lip twitched, but it was the only lapse in ceremony as she turned to give a swift gesture to the other guards. Two guards opened the door to the corridors, where several more stood at attention, then Maris led as Nim followed, sword at her hip. Bramwell, Wes, and the others fell in behind. In the corridor, they met Warrick, who stood in conference with even more of his men.

Warrick radiated power. He was tall and handsome and, for all that was sacred, Nim's husband. Even if only for the last few hours. He glanced up at her from beneath a dark brow, the silver coronet of a seneschal upon his head. Stewart's crown had remained with his body.

He will die a king, Warrick had murmured as they stood alone with him where he lay in state. They had both been awash with regret, loss, and the realization of the utter disaster that had unfolded upon them. He had taken nothing from Stewart aside from his signet ring. Warrick now wore it upon his finger after placing it there only hours before, when they'd watched Stewart burn.

Illness was not suffered to spoil the earth. No matter that magic had bloomed Stewart's lesions, his body had been destroyed by fire. The same as Nim's mother. She swallowed hard but held Warrick's gaze. He moved to meet her, turning so that the pair of them might walk the corridors side by side, the way that they would enter the hall as the future king and queen.

"Their Majesties—" the herald announced, leaving off abruptly at Warrick's look. No need for any too-specific title that might cause uproar before their coming pronouncements had even begun.

Nim drew a steadying breath. She felt Warrick's warmth beside her but not much else. He'd apparently decided to chain down the emotions that had to be roiling through him, and little wonder, given that his anger the previous night had revealed his secret to the world.

The hall smelled of perfumes and was crowded with warm, anxious bodies. Tension and tapestries hung throughout the space, a buffer to the sounds that might have otherwise echoed in Nim's ears. Warrick tensed, and Nim had to restrain herself from reaching to grasp his hand. The only things holding her fool feet from running out of the hall were the weight of the crown atop her head and the weight of his solemn presence beside her.

"Your Majesty," said a tall and richly uniformed man before the dais as he offered assistance up the stairs.

Her hands trembling, palms slick with sweat, Nim ignored the footman's proffered hand.

Upon the dais, Warrick gave the exchange a cursory glance before his gaze returned to the watching crowd. The courtiers would know they had no real chance to stand against him after the display of power that had knocked them all off their feet, not to mention that he had apparently suffered no lasting injury from the arrows that had driven through his shoulder and thigh. But knowing they could not win against him did not mean they would accept him.

She swallowed down a sigh, leaning into the warmth of Warrick's magic. No part of her wanted to think of the way he'd used his power or to consider how much it would change the future of Inara. He'd had no choice but to act, because of Nim. Because of what she'd done. Never mind that the crown fit her just a little too well, as if it had been made for her, despite that she'd only just learned she would be queen. It was impossible not to think of what Warrick had said about her being his partner—his equal—as if he'd planned for her to be his queen all along.

He might not have known what the Trust would do, but he'd known the end was nearing for Stewart. They both had. That was why the king had warned her away. But she'd not listened. Nim had wanted to save Warrick from the Trust.

She'd done no such thing, though. The important bit, she thought, was that Warrick had wanted Nim at his side. He had protected her. He was the only thing that had kept her safe. But thoughts of a broken contract and the knife wound in her belly that he'd somehow healed rose anew. She felt a strange twinge at the memory of Warrick wrapped protectively around her, his mother looking on. *Bound*, they'd said. She was bound to Warrick.

Nim glanced at the man beside her, the first king with magic in his blood. She did not know what he had bargained. She would ask him—just as soon as they crowned themselves king and queen of Inara.

CHAPTER 2

Nim stood beside Warrick at the center of the throne room, where Stewart had died only the night before. *Killed*, she reminded herself, taken by the Trust in their game for control. The kingdom outside would be in mourning. Not just for their king but their very way of life. But the courtiers before Nim and Warrick looked on with hatred in their eyes. They desired nothing more than Warrick's end. Their seneschal had betrayed them. As head of law and order for the kingdom, he'd been the very man responsible for keeping magic at bay. Even if it had been Stewart who'd demanded the laws, Warrick had enforced them. In every instance when a person had been hanged for association with the Trust, for dealings with those who held magic, the deed had been carried out at his direction. All the while, Warrick had held magic too. The citizens of Inara knew it.

And beside him was the outcast who'd been brought under the kingdom's protection, the girl they'd stripped of status. She'd returned as more than a mere daughter of a one-time king's advisor, but as a constable to assist Warrick. They had mocked her and scorned her, and now they would call her queen. They would have to bow to her.

She tamped down a wild urge to laugh at the absurdity. Then a sharp chill bit at her skin, and Nim's gaze was roaming the crowd. Warrick wasn't the only heir. Rhen was Stewart's heir as well. The queen had planned for such an outcome all along. The queen had plans still.

"Members of the court, I stand before you this morning with no promises of an easy time ahead." Warrick's voice remained steady, his gaze drifting slowly over the crowd. "My father, King Stewart, held his plans for the kingdom close to his chest. So that those who plotted against the kingdom and all it stands for could not prosper. So that Inara would not be brought down by those who wish to wrest control."

An unpleasant murmur whispered through the courtiers. Nim did not have to hear it clearly to understand they meant Warrick was one of *them*.

He spoke over the dissent. "We failed you, myself, the king, and his advisors." Warrick's gaze came briefly to Nim. "It was not the first time we have lost in our ceaseless battle with the Trust."

A hush fell instantly at his words, a collective indrawn breath among the crowd. No one had spoken of the Trust so boldly, not even Stewart dying upon his throne. And Warrick had more than minor ties to the Trust.

A strange feeling of delight swam to Nim from somewhere beyond the onlookers, and her gaze darted across the room, searching for its source. She did not see Calum or Rhen, but certainly if one were present, Warrick would sense it. He stood calm beside her, emotions and intimations locked tight within. Wesley stood before the dais with Maris, Warrick's guards posted only at the entrances. The seneschal's secret was out. There would be no need of guards to protect him when he could use his magic freely. The only thing Warrick needed to fear was the Trust.

But magic wasn't to be used freely, not truly. It always had a cost. That cost was why the queen hoarded it beneath the kingdom, why she stayed so close to the river of power that fed her magic. The scars on Nim's shoulder stung, as they always did, a constant reminder of the only sacrifice she'd ever made. She would do it again to save Alice, but she had never made a bargain willingly. Not until she'd tried to bargain with the head of the Trust.

"And as such," Warrick continued, "the kingdom must be secured. The walls will be sealed. No one will pass through our boundaries until the matter is settled."

Shouts of outrage ripped through the hall, their dissent no longer quieter than their anger and fear.

"The kings before have done all that was necessary to keep the kingdom safe, no matter the cost. That tradition will continue, not despite the cost Inara has paid but because of it."

Another round of shouting followed, but Warrick did not silence it. He only stood, appearing calm and steady as the tumult raged on. There was nothing they could do to stop it, nothing at all men and women of flesh and blood could do to stand against magic. Hands shifted to sword hilts, but the courtiers understood they could not win.

Warrick was not only their king. He held power in his very blood.

THEY LEFT the throne room to the unsettled crowd. During the final announcements, the crowd had seemed to grow slowly aware of the castle guard shifting at the exits as they prepared to deal with any uprising once Warrick's presence was no longer a threat. Gestures between the guard made clear that Warrick had already given instructions for the securing of the wall, for containing the citizens and dampening unrest. What he noticeably had not done was pronounce himself king.

Warrick barked orders to his remaining guards as he and Nim made their way through the halls. The guards stepped away to carry out their tasks, but Warrick's pace did not slow. When he finally stopped outside a room with a lock system that appeared to be as complicated as the one in the dungeon cells, Nim drew a much-needed breath. Wes and Maris were given their orders, and Warrick escorted Nim into the room alone.

She felt the warmth of his magic as the torches and candles lit throughout the space, throwing a soft glow over dusty shelves and disused furniture. Long floral tapestries in rich red and gold were scattered at random intervals over the smooth stone walls. The room appeared to be a study of sorts, though the cabinets bore locks, and the few chairs did not appear to have been crafted for comfort.

She let her eyes trail over the shelves only a moment before she turned to Warrick. Beyond him, half covered by draperies, was a painting of a long-ago king's conquest of a long-ago head of the Trust. Nim doubted the accuracy of such a scene—the Trust had surely gone underground by means other than a mere king's sword—which was likely why the art was hidden away. And because only a fool would tempt them to fight once more.

"This room is safe," Warrick told her. "We may speak at ease."

"I felt magic in the throne room."

He nodded. "Rhen."

"And you didn't stop him? You've locked down the entire kingdom, and yet he's to roam unchecked within these walls?"

"Nimona—"

She drew an involuntarily breath, her hand coming to cover her mouth as Calum's warning rushed back to her. The man who had promised to repay her had free rein to move about the kingdom, to use the magic of the Trust anywhere he pleased.

"They're no longer bound to the undercity." Her words were barely more than a whisper as she sat heavily on one of the carved wood chairs. "We've set them free." Her eyes went to his. "*I've* set them free."

Warrick knelt before her, taking her hands in his. "No. None of this is your fault. She has manipulated our fates since the beginning, forced us into this path and this path alone." He did not say her name, did not call her *mother*. Nim didn't think it was superstition; Warrick did not want to say her name for darker reasons. His thumb ran a slow line over Nim's palm. "She bound me from telling you, from telling anyone. You could never have known what she meant for us."

Warrick had to marry Nim, to be joined to her by a vow that superseded his vows to the king and his contract with Calum, before he could speak the Trust's secrets. Warrick had not been able to reveal Calum and Rhen were his brothers or that his mother was the dark queen who'd trapped her by magic. Nim had been forced to make the discoveries on her own. And every time Warrick had planned to tie himself to her by the laws of Inara, his plans had been thwarted by the king. Nim wondered whether Stewart would have allowed their union if the Trust had not been so against it. She wondered exactly how much the king had known.

The head of the Trust had clearly orchestrated far more than Nim had feared. Warrick's gaze met hers, his eyes unnaturally green in the light of a dozen magic-bought flames.

"When she agreed to your bargain, she knew that if you were bound to me, then you would be unable to bind yourself to Stewart with magic." Unable to save the king Warrick had been so long trying to protect. "That's why she agreed, why she didn't just let me die."

There was a strange sensation from Warrick that was gone too fast for Nim to make out. She didn't know if it was because the idea hurt him or because that was not the true reason the head of the Trust had allowed her to live. Maybe Warrick's mother had a use for her yet.

"Warrick, what did you give her in the bargain to save me?"

He let out a slow breath, his thumb still tracing the lines of her palm. "That Rhen would be recognized as my blood should I ever become king."

The sound that came out of Nim could not have been called

decorous, and the fact only made her more aware of the weight of her crown. "So, what? He's just allowed to live here? To come and go among court—among us—as he pleases?"

"No." Warrick's fingers tightened around hers. "I will deal with him. I've made no bargain beyond his acknowledgment, and that's no more than what he has already managed himself."

Unease settled in the pit of Nim's stomach. The head of the Trust had not wanted to give Warrick the deal. Nim had felt it and heard portions of their argument. Clearly, she'd wanted Stewart dead, which meant that the trade she'd made was somehow bad for her plan. "Why should she give up the bargain just to have Rhen recognized when Stewart's crown would first go to you—and if not you, then someone the Trust already had in place? Warrick, is she plotting to do to you what she did to Stewart—" Her words cut off at memories of the king. The same signet ring pressed against her hand now had been on Stewart's broken fingers only the night before.

"That would be poorly done," Warrick said, expression grim.

"Poorly done," she echoed. "But you cannot say she *won't*." Nim swallowed hard. "Because you vowed not to lie to me." Fates save them, it only grew worse and worse. "Tell me. All of the secrets out. Now."

Warrick stood, crossed to a tall cabinet, then unlocked the door. He came back to her, moving a chair so that he sat before her, and held out a palm to reveal a dozen thin silver rings. "Stewart was just a boy when they got to him." Warrick's gaze was on the metal that rested against his palm, his voice far away. Making him speak of someone he'd only just lost felt cruel, but there was too much at stake to wait any longer. "They lured him with a promise, with the security of knowing what his future held." His dark lashes swept slowly upward as his eyes met hers once more. He was so close, she could make out tiny fissures of darker color within the green. Those dark lines resembled eyes Nim had seen elsewhere, a hint of his father among a shade unnaturally bright.

"For the young son of a king," Warrick continued, "such a prospect was irresistible. But Stewart knew not to let them take his blood. He'd been warned what they could do should he be compromised. Gifts cannot be freely given, and so anything that they might take would have a price."

Nim felt sick.

"He was manipulated for years and, eventually, fell into one of their traps. When they had him, it was little work to draw him further and further in. They threatened everything that mattered to him. I suspect, at the time, his bargain with her seemed like hope. Like she would be his savior." Warrick wet his lips.

Nim could not judge Stewart. Yes, he'd been in line for the throne and had much to lose, but Nim herself knew the dangers of magic as well as anyone. And yet she sat with one of the most powerful of the Trust, wearing his ring and a crown. She reached out, brushing a fingertip over the silver rings scattered on Warrick's palm.

"He was given a prophecy of sorts, one that warned against silver and Moontide, of a betrayal by someone close to him, and the way in which he might lose his throne." His eyes came up to hers once more. "When anyone came into his circle, they were unburdened of their silver."

Nim felt Warrick's intimation that the entire room was full of such seized finery, each locked cabinet filled with trinkets that Stewart could not abide. There was nothing of magic in them, nothing that called to Nim, and the rings in Warrick's hand did not bite or sting at her touch. But Stewart would not have known—he'd lacked the ability to sense magic. He'd possessed only the fear of what was to come.

"But—" She felt herself worrying her lip and forced it free. "He was killed by the Trust."

Warrick made a noncommittal noise in his throat. "Bargains are rarely so straightforward as to allow themselves to be thwarted." He dumped the pile of rings on a small table beside him then drew the coronet from his head. He placed it on her lap, the silver bright against the dark fabric of her skirts. It was nothing more than a large silver ring glistening in the torchlight.

Nim went cold, her eyes snapping up from the coronet to Warrick. "You—fates take them—you think they made him believe it was you? *Your* betrayal?"

He shrugged. "It matters not. Nothing can be done to untangle their web of trickery now. They've taken him and, in doing so, what little trust he had in me."

It was disgusting. And ridiculous. And unbefitting a person of their power. "They cannot bargain such with him. That's not a prophecy. That's—" She managed nothing but a crude swear.

"Mmm," Warrick agreed. "Not more than anyone has come to expect from them, though." He gave her a look. "She did not leave the bargain without securing an heir and a spare, after all."

Something entirely unsettling rose from Warrick, an intimation that was so dark and filled with pain that Nim could make out no words, only the disquiet of the emotion. "And you," he said, "here now, with a prophecy of your own."

To decide the fate of the heir of Inara.

They were not pleasant words, but he hadn't said them to hurt her. He owed her the truth, she'd asked for it, and it was what she would get, whether it was agreeable or not.

Vow aside, he did not have to lie to her, because they were married. A niggling chain of thoughts surfaced—Maris's words, the magistrate, the hasty ceremony that had been followed by Stewart's demise.

Their vows had been spoken differently beneath Lady Sybil's instruction, though only by a few words. But words mattered. *Beneath stone and sky*, not *between*. *Beneath.* They were the vows that would be spoken by those of the Trust, whose magic rested below the foundations of Inara. Nim hadn't realized at the time —how could she have?—but it felt significant to be joined by vows that were recognized by both Inara and the Trust. It felt impossible that she was bound to Warrick by magic as well.

"What does it mean that I'm bound to you?"

He took her hand again. "It... means you are here." *Alive. Not bled out on the floor of an undercity chamber.*

She did not miss the hesitation in his words. The ordeal with his mother had been difficult for both Warrick and Nim. He hadn't been stabbed, though, so her sympathy on the matter only went so far. She needed answers. "How?"

"The binding allowed me to heal you without stealing from you a sacrifice that one who was dying could not pay." He'd explained before that a dying soul or a soul bound by contract who might never get free, that they would have nothing to give that was more valuable than their life.

"But magic always has a cost."

His nod was infinitesimal.

"So," she said, more sharply than a new bride might normally and with more than a pinch of dread, "how was my debt paid?"

"By my bargain," he said. "To acknowledge one brother and let the other run free."

Warrick's mother had bound him and Nim. He'd made clear with his threats that she was the only one who could. Which meant, ultimately, that the magic had come from the source, from the dark well of power that swam beneath the Trust.

Nim pressed a hand to her stomach, unsure whether it was a reflex related to the wound he had healed or that she might be sick. The magic that flowed in the pits of the undercity had never been given freely at all. It had been stolen by the Trust in their bid to accumulate power.

It had been taken from the desperate, the unwilling. Stolen from men like Nim's father.

CHAPTER 3

Before Nim had a chance to let the implications of the binding settle in, urgent knocking sounded outside. Warrick crossed to open the door, then Nim heard several guards explaining an issue on the square, that they knew he'd not want to be interrupted but...

Nim did not need to hear what wasn't said. The Trust. Dark magic. Warrick would have to go. Whatever else she might have decided to say would have to wait.

He returned to her and, lowering to face her, he squeezed her hand. "I must go." His voice was full of regret and low enough to not reach the waiting guard. "And you must not leave the castle."

She straightened, but the remainder of his warning was faster than her indignation. "When I am not at your side, you are to be accompanied by Wes. It's not safe anywhere inside the walls of the kingdom." His mouth turned down as he stood. "Not any longer."

Nim released his hand. "With Rhen traipsing about, it's hardly safe in my own room."

"You'll be in *our* room," he said. "And he's the least of our concern at the moment."

She stared up at him.

"His new diversion will keep him occupied for a while, in any case. The more pressing issue is the kingdom."

Nim bit down on her response. The citizens of Inara were facing what they viewed as a usurper king and the very real threat of the Trust. Warrick was right—neither of them was safe. At the moment, she wasn't sure anyone truly was. What mattered most in that moment was so much larger than the pair of them, but something inside of her could not seem to set aside the closer fear of losing him so soon. Nim stood, pressed a palm to his chest, and whispered, "Return to me. Unharmed, please."

"If ever I do not, it is only because I've no other choice." His words drove fear deeper into Nim's heart, but his parting kiss promised that he had every intention of seeing her soon.

HOURS LATER, she sighed as she finished the last of the hastily made lunch Maris had foisted upon her. Nim brushed the crumbs off the leg of her constable wardrobe, recalling how Maris had frowned when Nim changed out of the formal attire earlier. Though she'd allowed Nim to relinquish the blade for Wes's sake, her protector ensured the crown remained secured atop Nim's head. "You must show them," she'd said. "The kingdom has never been weaker than it is at this moment."

Nim did not argue that bad things had happened long before either of them were around, but she did acquiesce in the matter of the crown. What she really wanted was a very long nap. What she had was being queen.

"Nothing for it," Nim said to the empty hearth. "Best focus on what we can do." She glanced at Maris. "Escort me to the king's records, please."

Maris's mouth twitched at Nim's tone, but she only nodded then called to ready Wes. He popped through the sitting room door and stood tall, though his hand slid self-consciously over the front of what appeared to be a very new jacket and robe.

Nim stilled, her heart in her throat. "Wes, are those—"

He nodded solemnly. "Aye, my lady. Warrick has assigned me as king's advisor."

She drew a steadying breath to quell the emotion threatening to overwhelm her. It was the style of wardrobe her father had worn, that of a man who was closest to the king. Though his expression was unsure, Wes looked every bit an agent of the crown—outside of a missing sword. He was a lord, elevated far above the other courtiers. It was time to stop thinking of him as the boy who'd brought her a seneschal's messages. Wes had been through as much as Nim, and he knew well what was best for the kingdom. He was certainly the most loyal.

She gave him a sharp nod. "It suits you, Wes."

Color rose to his cheeks as he turned, proffering an arm to escort her from the room.

A few corridors later, they arrived at a stately office. An impressive number of the king's guard waited at the door as Nim led Maris and Wes inside. The room was large and well lit and appeared to branch off into a half dozen storage and document rooms, all of it done up in the finest detail while somehow managing to look elegant and imposing. Maris came to a stop beside Nim, hand resting on the hilt of her sword. "The seneschal's office."

Nim's gaze snapped to hers.

Maris grinned. "Where else did you think the king's records might be stored, Majesty?"

Nim walked forward, taking in the space with renewed attention, her gaze trailing over a wide desk of fine dark wood. Every inch of it spoke of the hours Warrick had spent poring over documents as part of his work for the kingdom. She could imagine him there, how exhausting and unwinnable it must have felt, and what he must have endured knowing his mother meant to destroy his father, Inara, and everyone he'd come to love.

Wes stepped closer, entirely unaware of her ruminations. "What can we help you find, my—Majesty?"

She let out a breath. "We're going to root out every person the Trust has sewn into this court. And when we find them—"

"Burn them to the ground?" The voice came from somewhere behind them, despite that the door had been set with an army of guards. The group spun to face whoever the voice belonged to. Maris's sword was already drawn.

"Rhen," Nim hissed. "You fate-forsaken spawn of a—"

"Please," he said with a gamesome grin and a courtly bow. His sapphire eyes leveled on her. "Call me prince."

Her gaze narrowed.

Rhen only smiled more earnestly, casually sauntering toward the desk, his route bypassing the sword Maris had at the ready. He picked up an iron from near the hearth and gave it a brief examination before moving forward again, as if his audience were not staring daggers and holding a literal weapon at him.

"What are you—" Nim's voice cut off as he threw her a wink from where he stopped in front of the desk. He waved the fire iron with a flourish then stabbed the center desk drawer with a firm jab that echoed a *thunk* through the room.

A massive serpent fell heavily onto the floor. Nim and Wes startled back. The cold, slithering sense of magic crawled over Nim as the snake coiled to spring at them.

Maris had not jumped back like Nim and Wes but immediately slashed out to dice the creature into several tidy pieces before it could strike. Nim would have to remember to thank her when her ability to speak returned. Rhen only inclined his head, as if the queen's protector had just graciously offered him tea instead of chopping up a serpent meant to attack, as if he were a social guest and not one of the very men who'd made her life torment.

Fists clenched and jaw suddenly tight, Nim took a step toward Warrick's brother. Wes grabbed her, yanking just hard enough to prevent a gain in momentum. If she'd had his sword at hand, she would have used it.

Rhen leaned forward on the iron, wrapping his hands about

the handle as if it were a cane. "Nimona, my dear, you do see that I have just saved you from certain peril, do you not?" He gestured vaguely toward Wes with his chin. "Though the boy might be able to save you from a direct attack by magic, he certainly has no power to prevent a serpent from puncturing your precious skin."

"As if it were not you putting the serpents in my path in the first place." She let the full force of her disgust seep into her tone.

Rhen sighed. "No faith." He straightened, tossing the iron carelessly to land with a clatter near the wall, then showed his hands in a gesture she thought must have been meant to prove his innocence. "Of course it was not I who placed the serpent in this desk. What would I have to gain from such an act?"

She opened her mouth, but no response found its way to him. Rhen had drawn his magic back, keeping his intimations safely out of her head. It felt as if he might be telling the truth, though she was not fool enough to trust it.

He tapped his nose. "Yes, there, you see. My best play is to stay safely on the gameboard. Warrick knows it, as well as the rest."

"Calum was in a cell when the snakes began popping up in my path."

He shook his head. "You are cleverer than that. There are far more involved than just my brothers and me." He cast a distasteful glance at the pieces of snake. "Though, to be fair, it's likely you're right that this was one of his." His eyes met hers again, something like concern behind their playful glint. "You have made quite an enemy of Calum. I can tell you from experience, he does not take well to being outmaneuvered."

"And you just happened to be here to prevent it."

His grin turned sheepish, though she knew it was only for show. "No."

Nim crossed her arms.

Rhen straightened, shifting forward slightly before Maris's

blade shifted as well. He gave them both a look. "I see that you've no intention of making this easy. So I shall come straight to the point. There is a power play inside the Trust. Secrets and treachery abound. I do not gain from such a game at all. As such, I would like to assist you with what information I can, let you in on what helpful tidbits I might." He leaned forward, tone conspiratorial. "For I have not been bound quite so exactingly as so many others have."

Nim had a flash of renewed anger, memories of Calum and the Trust and the violence they'd wrought, of the cruelty that did not just rest at the end of a cane but had extended through her life as even petty reminders of who she was, of how they had called her *miss* and tried to make her feel small.

Nim was no longer an outcast lady, though. "And why would you share such information with the queen of Inara?"

An intimation came from Rhen that was genuine delight at the turn in her tone. It said, *"Pride suits you,"* but his words were as casual as ever. "For my own benefit, of course." He gave her a playful look. "But would it be such a surprise that your needs and mine were aligned?"

"Yes." Nim's tone was level, and she was so focused on Rhen that she barely noticed the sound of the door opening.

"I agree," came a sharp, familiar voice, followed by the sound of the door closing once more and the vague sense of Lady Sybil's approach. "Quite shocking."

As the magistrate joined them, Nim did not take her eyes off Rhen. His gaze slid lazily toward the woman—one of his own kind and loyal to Warrick—in a polite but barely concealed appraisal. "Lady Sybil," he said with a bow, his intimation making clear he was entirely unsurprised by the interruption, "a treat, as always."

Sybil did not deign to look at him. "Majesty, how can I help?"

Pressing down the strange sensation of relief over support from someone who held magic in their blood who wasn't Warrick, Nim drew a steadying breath. "We are on a hunt for snakes." Nim glanced toward what remained of the snake then Rhen. "Thus far, we have found two."

Rhen's intimation was one of vexation. He cleared his throat.

Lady Sybil still did not look away from Nim. Head high, posture impeccable, she gave a swift nod. "Of course. I'll get to work straight away."

Nim was surprised that Lady Sybil had understood her plan so quickly, but before either had managed another word, Rhen leaned toward them. "Again, if I may—"

Sybil finally looked at him, her expression making painfully clear the sentiment *you may not*. Her narrow eyes seemed to darken. "I outrank you, *Prince*."

The words were laced with an intimation, the reminder of a time when such had not been the case, and Nim had the realization that Sybil had not just happened upon them in the seneschal's office. Warrick had raised her to the position.

An unfamiliar expression crossed Rhen's face before he flicked a glance at Nimona, apparently becoming aware that he would have to play their game. "Your Majesty," he said in the manner due a queen, "I can see that a show of trust is in order."

Maris made a sound that somehow encompassed the very soul of contempt. Her sword remained fixed where it waited to stab him.

Rhen's jaw twitched, but his gaze was steady. "You'll find a great deal of interest in Lady Brandon, I believe."

"I would sooner trust the night not to fall than to put my faith in you," Nim said. "Lady Sybil, please have this man escorted from my view."

Lady Sybil shifted, and the two eyed each other like a pair of cats before Rhen surrendered and inclined his head toward Nim. "As you wish. It is clear there are no inroads to be made here."

He walked from the room without a backward glance, and Nim could not help but remember their encounter with the head of the Trust. Rhen and Warrick had stood with Nim before the woman who pulled the strings as Nim worked out that Calum had earned the right to go free. Rhen's gaze had shifted to Warrick. "Besides," he'd said, "it's not as if our brother could not stand a bit of humbling."

She could not trust Rhen's intimations, but Warrick had not flinched at the conspiratorial look Rhen shared when speaking of their brother. Nim wondered if a bit of truth hid there, some sort of rift between even Calum and Rhen.

Moreover, the queen had not mentioned Warrick's involvement in the stabbing in the presence of the Trust guards. The moment they were gone, however, she had chastised Warrick for giving Nim the means to use magic against his brother.

Nim stared at the door through which Rhen had escaped, certain only that she could trust nothing she felt when he was near.

Maris sheathed her sword.

Sybil's voice was cold. "Lady Brandon will be dealt with. Leave her to me."

AFTER HOURS among the king's records, Lady Sybil chased Nim from the task with a debatably impertinent reminder that she was not likely to find anything the previous seneschal had not, with all his talents and a team of well-trained agents. Maris gave the woman a look, which Nim suspected meant the queen's protector quite preferred her charge rooting around in documents instead of whatever else she might get up to.

Nim straightened. "The both of you would do well to remember who makes the decisions here."

Wes yawned. "I fear that's the problem, Majesty."

He meant Warrick, the person who owned the loyalty of both Maris and Sybil. "You're right," she said, pushing to her feet. "Come, Wes. We'll find help with a few whose loyalty is, first and foremost, to me."

"Majesty," Maris started, but her mouth snapped shut at Nim's sharp look.

Shaking out his robe, Wes stood to follow as Lady Sybil—likely glad to be rid of the lot of them—returned to her work. "Where to?" Wes asked.

"Hearst Manor." The guard at the office door opened it quietly at their approach. "I've already received word from Margery. She's promised to scour the archives from the years before Warrick's birth." Warrick had sent men to retrieve Margery after the chaos of Stewart's death. Hearst was kingdom property, so Alice and Allister were safe there, but Margery's home had been protected by only a few of Warrick's guard. Nim's entanglement would make her friends targets.

The position she'd put them in was grievous, but Nim could not feel guilt for taking Margery from her home, not when leaving her there posed such a risk. She could only hope the access to documents Margery had never ranked quite high enough to obtain would ease the sting.

"We're not to leave the castle," Wes reminded Nim once they were in the corridor. "The kingdom is more than merely unsettled. Fights and fires are rampant, calls for hanging of nearly everyone among the court officials. Warrick has every entrance sealed." He leaned closer, voice dropping. "Even the few secreted ones I use to deliver messages."

Nim sighed, suddenly uncertain if Allister and Alice were safer where they were. Perhaps the castle, even though they would be nearer the target that was her as well as in closer proximity to Rhen, was better than outside. "Margery is already here. There is no one else I trust besides Alice and Allister." She glanced at Wes. "What of you?"

He shook his head. "It is you, and it is Warrick."

Grim-faced, they made their way back toward their rooms. A queen had duties, but Warrick had asked Nim not to attend public affairs until the unrest was settled, and citizens were not being permitted an audience in any case. They passed through an open corridor with the footfalls of a flock of castle guard echoing behind them. The dim light of dusk cast an orange glow over the stone archways, and Nim felt the familiar tug of magic deep within her chest. Her feet slowed, drawing her to the balcony overlooking Inara. Beyond the kingdom walls, thick fog had settled beneath a darkening sky. But inside the locked gates, lanterns and torches flared to life. Night would be upon them soon, and no lock on earth could keep Inara safe.

"What is it?" Wes whispered.

Wind whipped at Nim's hair, but Wes and Maris stood beside her, untouched, their cloaks still in the warm air. "Magic," she said. "The Trust is out there, before the night has even fallen."

Calum's bonds no longer prevented him from roaming the streets with his accountants, taking what he might from Inara's citizens. They had to be terrified, certain that a king who held magic was the end of all things, locked inside the walls and unable to escape what was coming.

King Stewart had upheld the law. No tolerance was given to citizens who associated with those who held magic in their blood. Bargaining for magical favors meant hanging. But all those whom Warrick had ordered hanged under the king's laws were not simply entangled with the Trust. Calum had been playing a bigger game with his bargains, forcing Warrick to fight small battles all over Inara. Warrick had freed Nim and Wes, along with many other children of Stewart's advisors, risking himself and the kingdom, while Calum watched from the safety of his position at the Trust.

While bound, Calum had done nothing but play games with Warrick. It was impossible to imagine what he might do once he was set free.

The draw toward the magic suddenly became stronger, so fierce that Nim found herself pressed to the balcony rail, her fingers gripping the cool stone. The dagger beneath her skirt screamed for blood, calling for sacrifice in answer to Warrick's use of magic.

It was Warrick, without a doubt. She could feel it as clearly as she felt the stone beneath her palms. And if he had been forced to use his power, Calum must be out there too, fighting for control of the kingdom with the magic of the Trust. He would not fight fairly. No one Warrick cared about would be safe.

There was a sudden sensation of warmth, flickering intimations she could not make out, and then the magic was sated, some sacrifice made in answer to magic's toll.

"Nim," Wes said at her whispered curse.

She turned to him, breath coming fast, skin alight with the desire to move. She could not stay hidden in her rooms, waiting to see what was to come. Fates save her, she was not made for that sort of tension. She needed to act. "Find Margery.," she said. "We need a plan."

Nim saw Margery—already dressed in slimly tailored working clothes as black as ink—off with a young scribe to assist in searching the archives. Her friend had vowed to lock herself inside until she found every single suspicious transfer and record of succession hidden there, along with any evidence of Trust associates inside the court. She was only gone a moment before Nim received a report that Lady Brandon had been removed to the dungeons for further questioning.

Wes gave Nim a look. "I don't like that Rhen was right."

She pushed away from the stack of documents they'd collected from the seneschal's office. "It was only to buy our trust. There's nothing they won't do to get what they want." She spun the ring on her finger, remembering how Calum had deceived her into trusting a magic key. She'd kept it on her person, close to her heart for years, never knowing it might someday do her in. Rhen would be no different.

"Wes, do you have the other contracts? Those Warrick rescued for the—" She swallowed hard, unsure what to name the victims of Calum's magic, certain she was not meant to speak of them at all. "The others like us."

His expression was solemn and a little weary, his hair a disheveled mess after their hours of work. "Most of the contracts were returned to their owners, but a few..." He shook his head. "A few were not well enough to take them back."

He stood to retrieve a stack of documents from a hidden compartment in a small table near the wall. When he returned to the desk, Nim could feel the sense of magic on the parchment, contracts like hers that had been bound by Calum and broken by Warrick's blood.

There were more than she expected. As she opened the first one, a soft breath escaped her at the familiar script, the binding words, the smell like cloves that lingered on heavy parchment. "How long has it been since Warrick won their freedom?"

Her voice was low, but in the quiet of the room, Wesley heard. "Years. He didn't..." He paused, and when Nim's gaze met his, he gave a little shrug. "I don't think Warrick knew about you. They must have somehow kept you hidden, made it seem as if your father's contract was still owned by your father."

"Until Calum sent me into a seneschal's private rooms." She frowned. Calum had made a bargain to keep Warrick from entering the undercity and the Trust. Nim could not fathom why keeping Warrick out had been important enough to Calum to trade his access to Inara, but that deal was broken. Calum was free. Her eyes snapped to Wes's once more. "Calum knew that Warrick freed the others."

Wes nodded. "He wasn't happy about it, for certain, but I believe his goal was only to drive Warrick to distraction. The more magic and energy he spent dealing with the Trust, the less he would have to secure the kingdom."

Nim had wondered if Calum's intent had been to see her hanged by the king. He was so filled with loathing for her, with promises of violence. But he must have known all along that Warrick would try to save her. Calum had brought her to his own rooms and asked her questions about Warrick and what she thought of the seneschal he'd made her mark. Clearly, he'd meant to use her against Warrick, but Nim wasn't certain how, given that the head of the Trust had tied her up in magic long before Calum bound her in a contract of her own.

Then Warrick had made Nim constable. The position had protected her by the laws of Inara, laws even the Trust were bound to uphold if they walked from their gates. And when Calum was locked in the castle dungeon, when he'd been unable to move against his brother or the king, Rhen had come for Nim. He had tricked her into walking right into his mother's lair.

They had used Nim to get to Warrick, after all, and in return, Warrick had vowed vengeance on his mother. Not Rhen. Not Calum. But the head of the Trust.

"My father's bargain was made with her," Nim said. Warrick's mother, the dark queen who held control over not only the Trust but its magic. Calum had tried to deceive a young Nim that she might have a chance to recover the debt, but it had all been a lie. He'd only wanted control. Nim's contract was broken, but the Trust still owned her father's contract. He could have never truly been freed; the man that he was had been devoured by magic long ago. And yet Rhen had taken her deep into the undercity, to a low, dark cell where something in Nim had recognized that it had once held her father. There seemed to be no reason to taunt her with it, not when he'd been taken so many years before.

She had felt Warrick's regret about her father, felt that King Stewart had preferred to hang those tangled in Trust business because what would have happened to them otherwise was far worse. It was a mercy, as unpleasant as it was, and it prevented the Trust from using the sacrifice of another man to add to their power.

A whisper of dread went through her. "If my father is truly gone, Wes, then wouldn't his debt be paid?"

Wes's brow pinched. "Perhaps it is now. It's been years since Calum trapped you in your own contract to repay it."

"Perhaps," she echoed, unconvinced. They'd taken her father, her mother, and Nim would never know how much else. If their lives had not covered the debt, she wasn't certain what else the Trust meant to claim.

As if guessing the direction of her thoughts, Wes added, "Your mother may not have been part of the payment, Nim. She may have only been punished for interfering."

He was right. Wes didn't remember his own parents, as they'd been taken by the queen when he was too young, but his father had made a bargain for the sword meant for Wes. And Wes had learned that many of the king's advisors had suffered the same fate as the king, succumbing to a mysterious illness. Slowly. Painfully. A warning from the queen.

Nim shook off a shiver of unease, looking again to the contract. The men and women close to the king had given everything in their attempt to save Inara. They had discovered Stewart's secret and, in turn, that Warrick was his son.

None of them had attempted to remove Warrick. "It seems odd, does it not?" She met Wes's hazel eyes. "That they left Warrick in his position, even as a boy, when they understood the hold the dark queen had on him."

Wes frowned. "He's a good person. He's..."

She nodded. Warrick had only been a child, and it was clear where his loyalties lay, but the kingdom had a long history of hanging anyone who posed a threat, no matter their intent or position. They hadn't tossed him into a cell, hadn't removed him from court. They'd done nothing aside from going all in on their own bargains to save Inara.

"Maybe they knew there was no use," he offered. "Perhaps they decided to fight her at her own game."

The contract was heavy in Nim's hand, the scent of cloves giving her a headache. "Perhaps they were right."

CHAPTER 5

Margery was no fool. Despite their new queen's orders to grant her access to the most protected of Stewart's holdings, there was no chance her escort—a guard gone white-haired at the temples who surely served under Stewart's father—was going to deliver her to a document that might have seen the previous king thrown into irons.

That didn't stop her, though, from following the escort. Margery had been welcome at court since she was a girl, and she'd dealt with their secrets for nearly as long. As soon as she'd learned her letters, she'd been stationed at her mother's side to aid in any way she might—fetching documents, copying notes, and giving one of several little signals should any visitors arrive unnoticed to peer at contracts they had no license to view. The courtiers' tricks had been obvious enough, sly words and manufactured accidents, anything at all that might give them leverage. Their desires had always been plain: more power.

But the beauty of power, true power, was that it rested in understanding.

"My lady," her escort said with a bow as the entrance to the archives was opened for them.

Margery gave the man a nod. "The guard can wait here."

She gestured for the young scribe she'd stolen from Warrick's personal staff to follow, the pair of them gliding silently into a room filled with towering shelves. A myriad of poorly trimmed candelabra lit the space, giving the scene the unpleasant sense of movement as flickering shadows jumped from shelf to wall. Empty tables rested in the center of the room, and several stairways drifted upward into the darkness of the levels above. The room smelled of ancient bindings and, inexplicably, of damp smoke, and it needed more than a simple airing out.

Margery glanced at the scribe. "Are you familiar with the layout, love?"

The girl nodded.

"Excellent. Choose a table, and I'll get you set to task."

Without hesitation, the girl did as requested, and though Margery was not surprised the seneschal had a well-trained assistant, she wouldn't have placed money on it, given what Nim and young Wesley had gotten away with under his care. She tamped down a smile, turning to examine the contents of the cases lining the wall. There was no question the kingdom held ample secrets.

Margery put the scribe to work with a list of tasks that would take even the most efficient of her sort days to complete, then she managed her own busywork for nearly an hour before her patience finally gave out. Truly, the archives held interesting information, but the urgency of Nim's situation made all else feel like a waste of precious time. Margery had wandered farther into the stacks, testing how long she might disappear before some hidden guard took notice, but it seemed they'd been left to their own devices. *Splendid*.

Hiking the length of her skirt, she slipped off her shoes, tucked them into a shelf, then sped stocking-footed up the dark stairs. Margery rarely made use of the many hidden passages threading through Inara castle, but she certainly understood how the courtiers that she wrote contracts and transferred property for moved from place to place, particularly when those transfers were from one courtier to another. Payment for secrets kept and services rendered could not be managed where an agent of the king might be discovered.

When she reached the top of the stairs, she slid a hand to the wall of the tower, not daring to light a candle that would have her found out. The stone was smooth and cool, the air still as she waited for her eyes to adjust. The dim light from below caught on only a few edges and hollows, but it was enough. As silent as the grave, Margery moved through the space to where two shelves rested in a shadowy alcove. She slipped her fingers over the edge of carved wood and polished stone until she found the shelf that sat just a hair farther back than the rest. Her hand disappeared into the darkness, grasping for the lever hidden behind a decorative pot. It clicked too loudly. She held her breath, waiting, but when no sound came from below but the whisper of paper, she pressed, cautious and deliberate, against the inset wall.

It slid open, allowing a meager space that forced her to turn sideways in order to slip through. She did not particularly like the sensation of being trapped in a narrow corridor, but she found herself pushing the shelf closed behind her nonetheless. The passageway was not as dark as she'd expected. Thin strips of light shone through from the opposite wall where it met the ceiling. She glanced in each direction with a new sense of appreciation for the sneaking that Nim had been forced into by the Trust. It was quite unpleasant, all things considered.

The floor felt like stone, scattered with bits of sandy mortar knocked loose from where the shelf nestled into its frame. She lifted one foot to shake off the worst of the dust then moved toward the more secure rooms of the castle. If Stewart had hidden anything, it would be under more than lock and key. It would be where no soul dared trespass.

Several sharp turns and musty halls later, she came to what— if she had navigated correctly—should be the magistrate's private office. Situated well behind the spaces used for ceremonies and guests, it was a small vault of a room with a passage leading to an actual vault room, which held a hidden sepulcher meant for the body of a king.

But the kings had been burned, not buried.

Margery pressed an ear to the door to the office, listening for any indication of movement inside. Given the hour, it was likely safe. She wasn't one to gamble when the stakes were so high, but fates save her, she didn't have time for caution. After only moments of silence, she released the latch, a soundless catch that she felt beneath her palm, and drew the door open to slip from behind a long tapestry into the dim room.

It appeared empty, but she'd taken only two steps when, in the shadows cast over the magistrate's chair, a figure moved. She froze, heart in her throat. The man glanced over his shoulder, his movement sharp and quick, bringing his face into the sparse light. For a moment, he froze too.

They stared at each other, though Margery was the only truly culpable party. She'd invaded the private office of an agent of the king. Surely Warrick would release her of any punishment, but he probably wasn't even on castle grounds at the moment. And she had a reputation to uphold. Discretion was everything when dealing with secrets—especially among the court.

She wet her lips. The candles had been snuffed, and the man appeared to have been on his way out, caught in a hasty movement that was halfway to *stand and leave*. One more minute, and she might have made it free and clear.

She resisted the urge to curse. Composure went far in such circumstances. "You must be the new magistrate." Her tone was one of unsurprise, and not too poorly done given the current situation. She did not recognize the man, but she'd heard Warrick had raised Lady Sybil to seneschal and was shifting his allies higher up the chain of command. That much she could count on.

He turned to face her fully, and she resisted valiantly questioning aloud how Warrick had hidden such striking talent from the court's gaze. He was dark-haired, his lean form moving with easy grace beneath a refined suit, the lines of his face distractingly well placed, even in the faint light.

His gaze followed where hers had briefly flicked to the chair, to the robe of his office draped over the back, then met hers again. Sliding a document into an inside pocket of his vest, he casually placed the other hand over the chairback and his robe. "And you are?"

"Margery." It wasn't as if a lie would play for long. If this man was to be magistrate, their paths would cross soon enough, and her true identity would be revealed. She'd well and truly stuck her foot in it.

"Margery," he repeated, the urgency she'd detected from him seeming to hover on her reply.

She gave a cursory dip. "Lady Margery Ayer."

His expression remained steady, but something seemed to sharpen in him, attention entirely on her, as if he'd recognized the name.

Margery was not surprised. She'd grown used to just such a response. Years before, her father had been among the most respected at court. One slip, one tiny whisper that he might have been involved in something unseemly, was all it had taken to stain his name. Never mind that the rumors had been true, those who'd accused and whispered had known nothing of the sort.

"Lord Ayer is dead," she told him. "You'll call me Lady Margery."

He smiled, a sudden and impish flash of teeth that put Margery entirely off her guard. "I will." His tone seemed to imply he intended to often.

Annoyed at the heat that swam to her cheeks, she turned her tone brusque. "I'm to assist in a task for the queen." What was the title Nim had given her again? Fate's sake, she had no idea. They'd rushed through much of what had happened, and after so many sleepless days, Nim hadn't made a great deal of sense.

"Hmm," he said.

Margery quite agreed, and she gave him a nod to say so, short and dismissive. She wondered whether she would be able to return to the corridor without him causing a commotion or if she might fare better striding past him to the main door. There was no way to steal into the sepulcher now that she'd gained his notice—no officer of the kingdom would allow such a thing. Not much was more sacred than a king's vault.

She'd not made the decision of precisely how to escape when he straightened slowly, as careful as if she were an animal renowned for spooking, then leaned on the edge of the desk nearest her. The office was narrow and dim, and his movement put them closer than she liked. Not that she minded the warm sandalwood and what might have been a trace of woodruff she was picking up from being so near him. But there was precious little time to be had, and certainly none for dealing with the inquisition being caught in the magistrate's office might cause. Perhaps she should send for Nim and simply have her clear the space. She was queen and could do such things, surely. Though it did seem a bit unsavory to involve Nim in such a damning task when she'd only just been crowned.

"Lady Margery, forgive me the impudence, but I'm afraid my curiosity is too severe to yield to manners. Or even good sense, for that matter." His voice was smooth, slipping like a spill of dark ink over stone, his interest fixed and plain. He wasn't even trying to hide it, apparently. He tipped his head forward, inching closer. "Why have you come in such a surreptitious manner?"

At least he had the grace not to out with the words *sneaking*, *secret passage*, and *at this unseemly hour*. She felt her chin rise just a fraction, regardless. "To bypass the line for admittance, of course. I was quite aware that today of all days, a new magistrate would have their hands full."

"Indeed." The hint of a smile played at the corner of his mouth.

She might have told him she'd only meant to pass through, but nothing awaited her beyond his doors other than a set of rooms she could access through any means—should one not count the vault.

Then his gaze trailed down her form with blatant openness to the hem of her gown—where just the tips of her stocking feet peeked out between dress and floor.

She cleared her throat.

Before she could form a rebuke, the man came fully to his feet, the motion bringing him closer still. Fates, he was tall. "I see," he said, as if the entire situation, stocking feet and all, suddenly made proper sense. "You've come to ask for my help."

That was absolutely not how she'd planned to talk her way out of the ordeal. Not at all. She opened her mouth to say so, but he cut her off again.

"For the queen," he said. "Of course, this should be our top priority." He straightened his vest, took another step forward, and crooked an arm out in offer. Light seemed to catch in his eyes, despite the dimness in the close room, sparkling like the reflection of a flame on restless water. "Come," he told her. "Allow me to escort you somewhere we might talk."

CHAPTER 6

The moon seemed to pass too slowly across the night sky, its light nearly faded when Warrick finally returned. Wes had fallen asleep in the sitting room, surrounded by pastries that Margery, who'd brought along her own cook when she'd been shepherded to the castle, had ordered made for him and Nim. She heard Warrick dismiss the guard in the corridor then carefully close the doors behind him to avoid waking Wes.

Warrick possessed a saunter like a wolf, a graceful confidence that spoke of his power. But as his eyes rose to hers, she felt something ease from him that was tinted with exhaustion and hopelessness. She was glad that returning to his rooms and to her had melted it away, but Nim could not deny her own unease at his lack of surety.

"My lady queen." His voice was low and a bit rough.

Nim sighed and stretched her arms, letting the unpleasant documents strewn on the desk go unsorted. She'd gained very little from them thus far, as it seemed every attempt at escaping bargain by the persons contracted had been thwarted by clever tricks and twists of fate. "Husband," she said back at him.

He stopped before her, staring down from an impossible

height as he took in what was most likely a well-disheveled wardrobe. His eyes met hers once more, warming something in her chest that slowly began to spread through her. "This was not how I meant to treat you as a new bride."

Nim raised an eyebrow as if in challenge.

A hum rumbled deep in Warrick's chest. "I suppose at the very least, I meant to be near you. If not the customs owed to you, to feast with your friends, to dance as husband and wife."

"Mmm," Nim answered, offering a hand to him. When he took it, she stood, her awareness of his magic and his nearness sending sensations through her like the fluttering of wings. "Our nearest friend has been stuffed with a feast of cake, and there is nothing to prevent us from having that dance."

One corner of his mouth lifted as he drew her to him. He had watched her dance with Allister at the masked ball, tied into a beautiful gown and bedecked with jewels. Warrick had wanted to dance with her as his wife then, had wanted to introduce her at court as his. But all that, he seemed to think, paled in comparison to the way she looked in that moment, rumpled and ink stained, alone in their rooms.

"Rumpled," she said with a laugh.

He bit his grin then leaned in to kiss her, the soft touch of his lips lingering before he pulled her to sway against him.

"You're right," she whispered. "I much prefer this."

Warrick's eyes were on hers, his intimations nothing but loyalty and devotion and vows too vast for Nim to fathom. But his thumb brushed across her palm where a deep scratch remained from their encounter with furious courtiers' arrows and blades, and he drew it to his mouth, pressing a kiss to the angry line. Heat spread through Nim, not simply from his touch, but with the sensation of comfort and warmth that always came with Warrick's magic.

She turned her palm in his, the flesh there suddenly smooth as though it had never been injured. Nim stopped swaying. She stared at the flesh then reached for Warrick's collar, tugging it loose to shove the material of his shirt aside to find his wound. His shoulder, where an arrow had torn through only the evening before, was clean, even skin. Her palm pressed to his chest, the thrum of her pulse matching his, beating in time with the magic.

She swallowed hard. He'd healed her in the space of a breath. *But at what cost?* She understood those of the Trust were not easily wounded. When Nim had stabbed Rhen, he'd been able to follow her under his own power to the gateway between Inara and the undercity. But when Nim received the same wound, it had nearly killed her.

"I felt your magic when you were out there fighting." Her words were barely more than a whisper, and Warrick's hand tensed at the small of her back. "It *wanted*, and I could feel it from here." It had demanded a sacrifice, the way that her dagger had craved Rhen's blood when they'd stood in the throne room. The magic had to be answered. The toll had to be paid.

He held her against him, his gaze never leaving hers. "I cannot be sorry for the effects our binding might have on you. Not when the alternative meant..." He shook his head, lifting his hand to slide along the sensitive skin of her neck, his thumb slowly tracing the line of her jaw. "I can only hope that it does not become unbearable."

Unbearable for whom? she meant to ask, but a new realization tumbled from the tangle of her thoughts. "It was not unbearable. In fact, I did not even swoon." Nim had been standing beside Warrick when he attacked Rhen in the throne room. His power had flooded the hall, strong enough to knock everyone from their feet, and she had not been taken by the swimming sensations that had always swept her away. She met his eyes again. "No more smelling salts."

The hint of a smile tugged at his lips from the awe in her tone, though Warrick's intimation made clear that he did not entirely feel as triumphant as she did. He'd done nothing but bring her closer to magic—to his mother and the Trust and everything that could hurt her. And yet her pleasure satisfied something inside him in a way that he could not deny. His eyes danced between hers, the warmth of his magic unfurling even more.

"No more salts," he agreed.

His fingers at the back of her neck urging her gently toward him, Nim rose to the tips of her toes to meet him in a soft, sweet kiss. It was so utterly and inescapably right that she forgot to wonder what else the bond might have wrought.

CHAPTER 7

Margery could feel time slipping away with the light of the moon. The magistrate had led her to a balcony overlooking a private courtyard, the sweet scent of early-blooming magnolia rising to them on a gentle breeze. Her hair had been drawn back into a heavy knot of braids, her working gown tight at her neck and wrists. But the dark hair of the man beside her shifted in the night air, his pale skin cast silvery in the dying light. She needed to gain the upper hand. She had no time to distract a magistrate and no desire to confess, even if he was someone Warrick thought he could trust.

"I really must—"

The man turned to her, interrupting her—unbelievably—again. "Lady Margery..."

He squared his shoulders in an almost imperceptible move, chest rising with a solemn breath, or she might have told him exactly what she thought of his persistence. His voice was low and even. "I must confess."

She stared at him.

He smiled, unabashed, then seemed to recognize the expression was inappropriate. He brought a hand to his chest, a silver band glinting on the finger that tapped against his breastbone. "I've brought you here not because—"

"My lord," Margery said in her sharpest tone, realizing that she'd yet to even gather his name. "Whatever you're about, I do not have time for it. If you would simply—"

He bit his lip, something about the gesture making Margery feel he was laughing at her. She had a good bit of savagery put back for courtiers who mocked her and was well prepared to unleash it. He must have seen it on her face, for he lifted his hands in surrender. Margery didn't tend toward sneers when she finally lost her temper, but instead a cool bearing that belied the ruthlessness she was about to set free. She was impressed that he seemed to recognize the danger he was in.

"You misunderstand," he explained. "The fault is all my own. It is only that I felt it was my duty to bring to your attention..." He glanced over his shoulder. "...that while I appreciate your legendary prowess in matters of court, the magistrate's office may not be the most secure place for you to discuss such things as a queen's task with me."

Not when it required ladies slipping about in stocking feet, his tone seemed to imply.

She felt her mouth twist down.

He inclined his head as if in another apology, but she still had the sense he regretted none of it. "I hope that here, we will be free to speak without interruption. And I, personally, will assist in any manner, regardless of what you ask of me, with the merciless expedience expected of my post." His eyes lifted to hers, brilliant glinting sapphires, his words a vow. "As I have sworn, above all, to be loyal to my queen."

CHAPTER 8

Nim stood alone in Warrick's study, looking out over Inara as the morning sun cast light on the damage caused by unrest and the Trust. Warrick had left in the early hours with far too little sleep, resigned to another day of fighting to keep the kingdom safe. Foreboding sat heavily on her chest. She'd heard snatches of the guard's report: fires, attacks on the king's men, and a hastily assembled gibbet near the square. Their reign was hanging by a thread, and the Trust was a thousand blades aimed to cut it.

She wanted to find Calum and his mother and stab them with her favorite dagger.

"Majesty," Maris said from beyond the door to the sitting room, "your tea has been brought up."

Nim sighed, the ache in her chest laced neatly beneath the constable wardrobe Maris was going to have a fit about. She reached forward, tracing a finger lightly over the glass. Warrick's magic thrummed through her, some enchantment that felt nothing at all like the magic of the Trust, that did not threaten to devour her but pulled her closer. Its pulse lulled her into a place that felt not calm but pleasant. Pleasant enough that she might linger just a while longer—

"Nim."

Wes's voice snapped through the room, drawing her back to find her palm pressed to the glass, her heart pounding in her ears. Nim snatched her hand away, unsure how long she'd been distant. It was out of habit more than anything else, the way she brushed her palm clean on the fabric of her overskirt before turning to face Wes.

His eyes stayed on her as if watching to see that she had herself under control. "Come," he said, "have some tea."

She did go, not looking back as they closed the door behind them, the magic-forged sword left resting on Warrick's desk.

In the sitting room, Maris stood before a low table that held the serving tray, her arms crossed, weapons sheathed. Her dark hair was pulled back, and her petite form was covered in a black uniform trimmed in black, featuring black accents. Something about Maris's pose made Nim think she also wanted very much to drive a blade into either Calum or the head of the Trust, but the queen's protector only inclined her head toward the tray.

"Thank you," Nim told her. "But I'd rather not—"

Maris's gaze flicked to Wes, who let out a rather peculiar sound of distress. Every other guard in the room—three, Nim noted, though there were likely more just outside—turned to look at him.

"I've just remembered," Wes said. "This is the absolute worst. I was to deliver one last missive to the new magistrate before Warrick was off." He shook his head, appearing to fight a blush at his failure to complete the task. "Bramwell, you'll have to run a message to Lady Pehn."

The look on the guard's face said plainly such was not the case. Regardless of Wes's new station, Bramwell's orders came from the king.

Maris made a noise of disapproval. "He'll not be able to leave the queen's side, your lordship. And you are to remain with the queen."

Both Maris and Wesley looked at Nim, waiting, apparently,

for her to respond. She glanced at the tea tray, the guard, then back at Wes. "I would be happy to take a turn through the garden. Perhaps we could drop the message off on our way."

A sigh eased out of Wes, and he took her arm, leaving no room for further argument. "I just need to pick up the missive from my study. It won't take but a moment."

Bramwell's sharp gaze moved from Wes's grip on Nim to Maris, but the queen's protector only gave him a bit of an eyeroll, her hand easy on the hilt of her sword. He turned to follow as the group made their way into the corridor. Wes's arm was noticeably unsteady as he took them to his seldom-used suite near where other agents of the king resided.

He stopped at the nondescript door and turned to face Bramwell and the guard. "You can wait here. No room for all of us inside. Besides, Maris will surely be enough."

Maris gave Wes a look but only shouldered past him into the room, her posture still at ease. The moment Nim had entered behind her, Wesley closed the door and secured the lock.

"What in the name of—"

Cutting off Nim's words, Maris ushered a wight from beneath the desk. It was not a creature; it was Alice.

"Majesty," she gasped, falling into a curtsy so low, a few stray locks of her wild auburn hair nearly brushed the floor.

Nim rushed forward to gather the girl into her arms, but Maris was faster. "No time for that," Maris said in a hushed tone, urging Alice to stand. "Tell her, quickly before the guard realizes what we're about."

Nim's gaze was darting wildly between her protector and a bedraggled Alice, realizing the girl must have refused to speak to anyone but Nim. Alice's clothes were well made, the uniform of her new station at Hearst Manor and in employ of the kingdom, but she looked as if she'd had a run-in with a sickle-wielding chimney.

"Majesty," she said again, her tone as frantic as Nim had ever heard it. "We were told to stay inside, under guard, and we did just what Warrick said. He's king now, and you know well and truly that we would only do as proper. I went to my room after dinner and locked myself inside. We don't have to lock the doors, but I've done so ever since *he* came, just in case—"

Maris's hand on the girl's arm had become less of a grasp and more for support, but she nudged the girl in a gesture clearly meant as *quicker*.

Alice gave her a glance then looked back at Nim. "I thought it must be that he didn't wake," she said. "He's always down to the kitchens before dawn. Before even me."

Cold dread settled in Nim's stomach.

"I was sure he was only in his room. If I hadn't thought, I never would have waited. You know I would have come sooner."

Allister.

"He's gone," Alice said.

"Was he—" Nim's gaze shot to Maris, confusion and fear tripping over one another in her mind. She did not know how the Trust might have gotten to him. "Have they done this?"

There was no way Trust accountants could have made it through Warrick's guard, not without someone alerting the king. However they'd reached him, whatever had happened... Nim swallowed hard. Only one person was capable of such a feat, and it did not bode well for Allister's safety. She looked back to Alice. "Since last night?"

Alice passed Nim a crumpled letter. "This was in his room. Some nonsense about his aunt and that he would be back by the turn of the moon." Her green eyes narrowed. "I knew it was wrong. It felt off, like the dress he sent you."

Calum, she meant, Calum and the dark magic of the Trust. Nim took the parchment and felt what Alice already had, the wrongness and a lingering scent of magic, dark and sulfurous, layered beneath something reminiscent of cloves. Beneath it, the sense of regret and a strange tingle that drew Nim to press her fingertips to the ink. Alice stood waiting, wanting more than anything to have Allister back. Wanting it so much that Nim could feel it.

"Allister..." Nim's voice broke, and her knees felt weak, but something pressed her forward, near enough to touch Alice's face. "You want him returned," she whispered.

The girl's brows drew down, because she obviously did, and no one seemed to understand what Nim was saying. She could feel it somehow, sense what the girl desired. Nim leaned forward, tugging the girl into a hug as her hands shook. Earlier, with Maris, and before that, Wes—fates take her, but Nim could sense what each of them wanted.

Because the magic craved sacrifice. It knew what those around her wanted. For all things sacred, she was in over her head.

She pushed back enough to look Alice in the face. The girl must have found a way past the guards at Hearst Manor. Nim had no idea if they were aware of her escape. "One thing at a time," Nim said firmly, though she felt nothing of the sort. "We find Allister." Her gaze returned to Maris and Wes. "We find Calum."

She let out a ragged breath. Calum had done this. She would kill him herself.

"STAY HERE," Nim said. "I'll get the sword, and then we take Alice to—" Nim shook her head, glancing from her protectors to the girl. They were in a mess, and they needed help. Bramwell was outside with a band of guards and an order from a king. Nim would be forced to wait until Warrick returned before she or her friends could act.

"I'll go with you," Alice said. "They can't have figured it out by now, or half the king's guard would be on my trail."

"They'll know soon enough. If the Hearst guards figure out you and Allister are missing, they'll warn Warrick, and the sooner, the better. We need him." She'd made a mistake in acting without him before. She wouldn't do it again.

Alice shook her head. "We can't let the guard find out." She pointed to the missive in Nim's hand. "Calum left the letter for us. For you. If the rest of the Trust knows we're onto them, then we will never get Allister back. They'll just use him against Inara. Like last time."

Nim stared down at her, prepared to explain that what she was saying was impossible for so many reasons, not the least of which that news of two missing agents of the king would not stay quiet for long.

Alice shrugged. "I made two new letters. It honestly wasn't a half-bad idea. One from me and one from Allister. I wrote that we ran off together, because we got scared, felt threatened by the Trust, and would return when the kingdom was settled." She brushed a loose lock of hair away from her face. "I left a passage door off its hinges, just enough. They'll think for certain we went through there." Her small face twisted as she seemed to consider. "By my wager, we've about half a day."

It wasn't enough, but Allister could wait no longer. Whatever happened to him, it would be on Nim.

"Very well," she said. "We go." They would just find Warrick on their way. They would send a message, whatever it took. They would stay outside of the undercity and out of the Trust's reach. This time, she would do it right.

"Your guards will not be such an easy slip, Your Majesty."

Maris's pointed remark did not go unnoticed, but Nim could only sort one thing at a time. "We'll deal with it. First, the sword."

"Bramwell," Nim said as she swung open the door. "I'm off to my room, as I've just remembered I left my sword. If you'll excuse me."

He inclined his head slightly, stepping back to allow her escape. The moment she was through, though, the giant of a man reached behind her, grabbed Wesley by the shoulder of his tabard, and yanked him out after her.

Nim swung to stare at the guard. Wesley was a lord. He was not to be tossed around like a prisoner—

The look on Bramwell's face finally registered, just as the rest of the guard closed rank and the door was slammed closed with Maris still inside.

"No," Nim hissed.

"Yes," Bramwell said as one of his men turned the key in the door's lock. "I'm afraid, Your Majesty, we've been given very strict orders should any agent of the king seem about to commit treason of any sort."

Wes groaned, seeming to crumple beside Nim. They'd been caught before they'd even started.

Her gazed flicked to Wes then back to the guard. They hadn't known about Allister, surely, or someone would have heard. If nothing else, Nim would have noticed unusual movement of the guard. What the guard knew, then, she had no idea. At the very least, Bramwell understood that the lot of them were planning something.

"You're to stay with the queen until His Majesty returns," he told Wes. The statement seemed to imply that Wes's power to keep Nim safe from magic was the only thing keeping him free.

That meant the guards didn't know Alice was in the next room. "When will that be?" Nim snapped. "When does Warrick return?"

Bramwell sighed. "I'm not going to send a runner after him just because the two of you—if you'll pardon my bluntness, Your Majesty—can't stop from getting up to endangering yourselves." Nim felt her shoulders draw straight, and he added, "The kingdom is in great peril, Majesty. They *need* Warrick out there."

Allister needed Warrick. She took a step forward, voice going cold. "I am your queen."

He dipped his chin, the gesture solemn and entirely deferential. "With respect, my queen, the kingdom comes first."

Behind the door, Maris made a sound that could be taken as either *unlock this door or I will run you through while you sleep* or *as queen protector, my duty is to place queen over kingdom*, depending on where one stood.

"Let her out," Nim said.

He stared back at her, unmoved.

Her jaw pressed so tight, she felt as if it might crack. A glance at the rest of the guard told her she had no chance at persuasion. Allister was trapped somewhere, captive of the Trust. Calum was cruel and brutal; he would remember the stand her friend had taken when fighting in her defense. Allister would be paid back for smashing the serving dish over Calum's head. He would be hurt because it would hurt Nim. She could not leave him. She could not wait for Warrick.

Nim was no longer powerless. The guard might have to protect Inara, but they could not harm its queen. She shoved past the guard, Wesley hurrying after, and the lot of them turned to follow. Not looking back, she strode straight to her rooms, to Warrick's suite, then burst through the sitting room door.

The sword was gone. She let out a nasty curse.

"Nim," Wes whispered, but she didn't waste time explaining.

Being near the sword would have hurt Wes in any case. She needed something better. Something just as strong. Something that could fight magic and that her other protection—the young man at her side who made them impervious to magical attack— could be near without harm.

A grim expression surfaced along with an even grimmer plan, and Nim was moving again. The bedroom door opened to dark- ness, but she did not need the light. Warrick's sparsely decorated room held little more than a bed and wardrobe, and she found the chest of drawers without so much as lighting a candle. The drawer slid open, and she tossed the blanket aside.

Behind her, Wes gasped, though she wasn't certain whether he could recognize the magic or just understood the horror she was about to commit.

Calum's power surged through her the moment Nim's hand wrapped around the cane.

CHAPTER 9

Dawn had risen over the balcony hours before when Margery had surrendered her trust in the matter of the king's vault to the magistrate. He'd taken to her plan with an unexpected eagerness and no hint of censure. He'd only begged leave for a few short moments, during which she'd considered bolting without him—and given up only because she'd left her shoes in the archives with what she hoped was a very busy scribe. Then he'd returned with a promise that he had removed the guard and any potential onlookers from their path. With that, Margery's fate was sealed.

She had argued that he did not need to actually escort her into the vault, but he would hear none of it and drew a set of keys from his waist pocket, assuring her the king's rooms were not as easily accessed as one might presume. Margery presumed nothing. She had a matching set of keys tucked inside the pocket of her gown.

By the time they'd locked themselves inside, lit the room's torches, and slid aside the large stone lid that topped the sepulcher, Margery and the magistrate had fallen into companionable cooperation. She had informed him they were looking for a contract regarding a young Stewart and nothing more. Should he find anything of the sort, he was to hand it to her for inspection.

King Stewart had not been the first king to use the sepulcher as a vault, however. Among a few scattered trinkets and jewels were a hundred scrolls and ledgers, ancient parchments inked by the forebears of Inara. Surely most were incriminating in one way or another, or else the documents would not have warranted such a secretive home. Margery found herself lingering on the text of a will, the last wishes of a long-dead king. The words were so privileged, a king's scribe had not even been permitted to pen them. Feeling a bit like a trespasser, she glanced at the man beside her and found his mouth soft in apparent amusement.

"What is it?" she asked.

Her voice was quiet in the stillness of the room. His features were lit strangely by the two short candles centered on the floor between them—where a pair of agents of the king had settled themselves in a nest of dangerously confidential parchment to search out secrets that might see them killed. Margery hadn't enjoyed herself so much in weeks.

The magistrate was looking back at her, the edge of his lip tucked just beneath a row of teeth that seemed perpetually ready to escape in a smile. He tilted the page away from her. "Lady Margery," he said, as that was all he had called her since she'd demanded it of him, "I'm afraid this missive is far too indecent for the genteel. Why, even I find myself shocked, and I'm only passably respectable."

"Passably. By whose estimation are you only passable?" He was the magistrate, after all, one of the highest posts in the kingdom. A man of his station was required to possess an unimpeachable reputation. Never mind that he'd been appointed by a Trust heir, that he sat amid documents no one—agent of the king or not—had leave to view, and that his accomplice was in stocking feet.

"Oh, mine, of course." At the tilt to her brow, he tugged the letter farther from her view. "By my own assessment, I am entirely adequate of both character and charm, no more."

Her laugh surprised her. The look he gave her in return surprised her even more.

"Lady Margery, I can honestly say that your violent entrance into my path has been an unanticipated delight."

The feeling that skittered through her could not be called unpleasant. If anything, she was perilously close to enjoying it too much. She straightened the stack of parchment in her lap. There was not a single window inside the vault, but given the hour she'd stumbled into his office and the way her legs ached from lack of movement, they must have worked well into the morning.

"I'm sure I'm keeping you from your tasks," she said. "Truly, I can finish up here—"

He put his hand over hers. "I wouldn't dare leave you to this alone."

His skin was warm and soft against hers, the quiet confidence in his tone a reminder of how intimate the space had grown. She needed to end this, whatever it was, but her reply was cut short—not by the magistrate, for once, but by muffled shouts somewhere outside the thick stone walls.

He did not so much as flinch, his gaze not snapping to hers or to the door as one might expect. He only appeared resigned, as if he might be disappointed the moment had ended. It was the same look her cousin Beasley always got when he'd met the end of his luck at cards.

"My lord," Margery started, but he stood, graceful and swift, the letter he held falling with a whisper to the floor near her feet.

She stared at it. It was not the intimate love letter he'd hinted at at all, in fact, but a neat column of figures.

A lie.

Her gaze snapped back to his.

He sighed, tugged his vest straight, then pressed a palm to

his chest, tone earnest. "Lady Margery," he said, dipping toward her in what was more respect than she might technically be due, "it is with great pain that I commit any act against you."

Margery shoved to her feet, but he was too fast. His eyes met hers beneath a dark brow, something unearthly glinting in their depths. He was at the door before she could act, slamming it closed behind him with the sickening click of a lock sliding home.

Margery stood in shock amid the precious documents, staring at the heavy door. Gone was the man who'd trapped her.

Outside, the deep voice of a palace guard reported, "The queen has taken up arms."

CHAPTER 10

Nim stood outside the door to Wesley's study, cane raised high. She wasn't certain precisely what the magic in the weapon would do, but neither was the guard.

"Open it." Her voice was cold and steady, the command of a queen. Her hands, however, were slick with sweat and trembling with the force of power running through them. It was a stinging, burning heat that throbbed with her pulse. It *wanted*, and it wanted badly.

"Majesty," Bramwell said again, one hand on his sword hilt, the other out in a gesture of supplication. He would not draw his weapon against his queen, but he could not let her go.

She didn't care. She was leaving. "The door," she demanded. "Now."

Wes's gaze flicked calculatingly between Nim and the head of Warrick's guard, then he edged forward and snatched the key from Bramwell's hip. "Got it—"

Nim shouted another warning to keep the man, twice as thick as poor Wesley, from snapping him in two. Garrett and several other guards whose names she could not bring to mind shifted closer.

Nim prepared her swing. "Not another step."

They would not move on her, but she could see in their eyes they had every intention of stopping Wes. Their allegiance was to the kingdom, and before them stood Nim, wielding the magic of the Trust and acting against king's orders. She must look like a madwoman.

A bark of wild male laughter sounded as if in response to the thought, and Nim turned, prepared to release the magic humming through her, warm and ravenous.

At the entrance to the corridor stood Rhen, hand to his chest and a cheerful if startled expression on his fate-forsaken face. "Your Majesty," he breathed. "You never *cease* to delight."

Nim cursed. Rhen's presence was the last thing she needed. He seemed to take in the scene, his eyes landing on the door to the study just as a solid *thud* sounded from the other side.

"I have the key," Wes said toward the door.

Another *thud* seemed to answer that he was taking a bit too long. The frame was solidly done, though, and the door was not apparently quite as eager as Maris trapped inside.

Rhen's lips pressed hard together in a pinned-down smile. He made a sound of approval, apparently at the current state of affairs, just as another door slammed open down the hall. Three robed officials strode through, coming toward the group: Lady Constance, Lady Lora, and a third woman whose dark curls were tied back above the tight collar of an immaculate black dress.

Rhen made another sound, this one slightly strangled, and when all eyes were back on him, he let loose a small stream of magic. Nim felt the ribbon of power tickle past her senses just before the lock on the study door clicked softly.

She stared at Rhen, certain no one else could be aware of what he'd done and unsure what, precisely, he was about. He tapped a finger to his nose, and she suddenly felt a little ridiculous to be wielding a magical cane over her head. But honestly, she had no time for poise.

Give me Allister, she thought at him as hard as she could, her grip tight on the cane.

Rhen only stared back, evidently unaware she was attempting some sort of intimation magic. "My lady queen," he offered at her expression, "may I be of assistance to you?"

Wes moved closer as if a magical attack might be imminent, and Bramwell shifted in front of the door. The door swung open behind him. Bramwell fell in, and an unrestrained Maris kicked him heartily in the chest before leaping over his prone form and into the corridor, sword drawn. Her gaze flicked between the cane over Nim's head—which did not help how ridiculous Nim was beginning to feel—and back to Rhen, who inclined his head gracefully.

Before anyone could get another word out, Lady Constance entered the fray. "Majesty." She dipped into a curtsy while the two women behind her followed suit.

Nim lowered the cane to shoulder height. "Lady Constance, I—"

The woman waved a hand. "It is of no consequence, Your Majesty. I trust that you have every right."

Rhen's tongue pressed his cheek, but he said not a word. She had the sense he wanted out of the corridor as badly as the rest of them.

"Yes," Nim said in response to Lady Constance, shoulders straightening as she gave Maris a meaningful glance. "Now, if you'll excuse us, we were just going."

The guard closed rank. Bramwell, on his feet now, shouldered closer to the newcomers. "Ladies, if you please, remove yourselves from this corridor at once."

Lady Constance, Master of Coin, shot a look at the guard. "Bramwell, dear boy, have you met the new magistrate?" She gestured to the dark-haired woman of rank behind her—despite that Nim ranked higher than any present and had failed to gain the upper hand. "Lady Pehn."

Somehow suddenly beside Nim without her having noticed, Rhen cleared his throat.

Nim startled, lifting the cane again as if to club him.

"Majesty," he said gently, "perhaps we should go."

An impatient huff of air escaped her. "I am trying." She did not outright call him a buffoon, but her tone was plain enough.

Louder, Rhen said, "Very good. Allow me to escort you." He put out an arm, but Nim ignored it.

The swords that were drawn took aim at Rhen and his proffered arm. His eyes pressed closed, and he stretched his neck.

Lady Constance stepped forward, through the gauntlet of swords, to stand before Nim. "Fate's sake," Lady Constance said, "this seems to have gotten out of hand. Can I interest you in taking a moment to rest in my rooms?" She nodded to a line of doors down the corridor. "It's just over there, and I've had fresh tea readied."

Nim did not want tea. In fact, she'd left hers cold in Warrick's study, and she certainly did not want rest. She wanted to take the cane thrumming in her hands and smash it over someone's head. Repeatedly. It was precisely that feeling—and the tone with which Lady Constance had spoken—that allowed her to lower the cane.

"Yes," Nim said, straightening. "Tea sounds like just the thing."

Wes, Maris, Nim, and the ladies Constance, Lora, and Pehn assembled around a small table in Lady Constance's elegant sitting room, not drinking tea. Rhen, Bramwell, and a good portion of the king's guard stood waiting outside the room. Alice, fates save her, was presumably still hiding in Wes's study beneath a desk.

Lady Constance's silver hair was drawn into a sleek knot at the nape of her neck, the robes of her station draped over a chair. Her attention rested on Calum's cane for a long moment before her eyes, as sharp as ever, came to Nim's. "Now," she said. "Tell me what has happened."

Trapped and exhausted, Nim resigned herself to the truth. "They have Allister. Alice, the girl who accompanied us to the ball and shares charge with him at Hearst Manor, came to warn us. She brought us a letter that makes clear he was taken by the Trust."

Constance's expression did not falter, but Lady Lora looked unwell.

"She's afraid if we tell the guard that Allister has been taken, Calum will use the situation against the king." Nim sighed. "I'm afraid she's right."

Constance nodded. "Aye. And you're not able to leave under watch and guard."

She shrugged. Queen or not, Nim was bound by the law. Inara came first. The kingdom was locked down. Warrick had clearly done so for just such a reason.

Gaze snapping sharply from Wes to Maris then back to Nim, Lady Constance said, "I have your word that you'll take precautions? That you'll warn someone outside the castle once you're clear of the guard?"

Nim went still.

The lady waited.

"I can't—I've just told you we can't walk out the castle gates with a flock of guards on us."

"My girl," Lady Constance said, "I am as old as sin. Do you think I do not know a thing or two about this castle your young Warrick does not?"

CHAPTER 11

A quarter hour later, they burst out of the hidden corridor beneath a low castle wall behind the bakery, gasping for breath. It was little wonder Warrick knew nothing of Lady Constance's secret route—the space was so narrow and starved for air, Nim doubted anyone would believe they could even get through.

Wes was doubled over beside her, Maris frowning as she wiped something dark from the shoulder of her uniform.

"Well," Nim managed, but that was about all.

Maris made a sound of agreement then leaned forward to test the weight of a metal rod near a selection of what might have been stove parts. She handed the rod to Wesley. "Not a sword."

He looked at it, unconvinced. His hands were gloved, the fine black leather stark against the ash-coated scrap of iron. Beneath the material, his fingers were covered in magic-wrought scars.

"Take it," Nim said. "I can hear the fighting from here. You should have a weapon."

They stood for a moment, hidden from the midday sun in the shadows of an overhang, listening to a kingdom in chaos beyond the workings of everyday castle life. The tightness in

Nim's chest had not eased for ages, but now she felt as if a band was being twisted around her lungs.

Calum, it screamed with every wrench tighter, *Calum, Calum, Calum.*

"Let's go," she told Wes and Maris. "The last thing we want to do is face him during the night."

Maris led them along a route that went first toward a storehouse then crossed to a cistern before she stopped to count the guard. Constance had evidently known her business, for the way was nearly clear.

While they waited for a sentry to pass on the wall opposite them, Wes leaned in to whisper to Nim, "What do you think you can do with the cane?"

She took another shallow breath. "I don't have the faintest idea, but I suspect neither of us will like it."

He nodded. "I suspect it will have a cost."

Nim turned her face toward his, but Maris interrupted with a hissed command to rush across the open space. There was a distant shout from the gatehouse, an order to take up arms, and the castle guard was suddenly at half force while the rest rushed to deal with an apparent threat. Nim and company made a harried run full of close calls all the way to the outer wall. Then they were free, outside the safety of the castle and its guard. Nim felt the loss of it.

She'd left her crown on Constance's tea tray, and though her wardrobe had been made by the kingdom's best tailor, it felt like nothing as much as the wardrobe she'd worn for years during her work for the Trust. But Calum no longer owned her.

Crown or no, Nim was still queen. And she was going to walk right into his territory and bash him to death with his own cane.

Wes laid a hand on Nim's trembling arm.

She shook herself, drawing back from the desires of the magic. "Yes," she told him. "Send a message with the first trustworthy soul you can. Then send another as spare."

They had to warn Warrick. She had to find Allister.

Wes found a messenger and a familiar guard from the watch to search out Warrick. Neither had his whereabouts, but someone of the king's repute wouldn't be difficult to track down. It only made Nim more aware of her own standing.

Despite the warmth of the day, she slipped her thin hood over her dark hair. Wes and Maris were not exactly inconspicuous, but Nim doubted the mere sight of either would bring calls for a hanging. She could not say the same for herself.

Evidently, the people of Inara had ample distractions to keep their attention otherwise occupied, though, because not a single eye turned to the group. Maris, out front with her sword free from its scabbard, kept close to the buildings regardless. Through narrow alleyways and past shops that should not have been closed so early in the day, they moved as if at any moment, the stones of the kingdom might be pulled from beneath their feet.

"There's nothing for it," Maris said, voice low. "Too many routes are blocked. We'll have to cut through the square to get anywhere near the gateway or Hearst."

Unease swam through Nim's gut. Hearst was near the entrance to the undercity, because that was where Calum had wanted her when she'd been tied to his bargains. She should have known better than to leave anyone she cared about there, no matter that the manor had been seized as kingdom property. Allister and Alice had never been safe, and it was her fault. She hoped Lady Constance had rescued Alice before the guard discovered the girl.

Wes's hand brushed Nim's back, and her resolve firmed. "Do it."

Without so much as a backward glance, Maris was moving again, swift and sure. She had the lethal grace of a cat on the hunt, her steps falling deftly into place around wash puddles and bundles of rush as she weaved her way through passersby and between obstacles.

The square was lined with king's men. Beyond the shopfronts

stood king's guard and watchmen alike, dispersed in even rows that blocked the scattered people milling about from moving through the center of the square.

"They're keeping a crowd from forming," Wes whispered. "Easier to control."

"Harder for the Trust to hide." Maris's chin jerked to a shop across the way.

A wiry man in a black suit leaned casually against the building, a cane not unlike Nim's in his hand.

Nim swallowed hard. The air was close. Long banners hung heavy above the square, the sounds of the shop work echoing dully off storefronts and stone. It appeared as if the kingdom was caught somewhere between decorations to celebrate Moontide and to honor the loss of a king. It appeared as if it was not the Inara she knew at all.

She could feel lingering power all around them, catch the scent of magic and the sense that it had recently been used. And if the Trust accountants were using magic, then they were taking sacrifices—freely and without repercussion.

But it was not simply the small magics of the accountants that she felt. Something stronger swam beneath it. Nim's boot splashed into a wet drain, and she froze, a staggering, familiar sensation searing through her. She'd not realized she'd been moving; Wes's and Maris's eyes were on her.

She'd felt it before, the draw so strong that it seemed tied deeper than her own will. It had been when Warrick and Calum had faced off and played their powers against one another.

It was Calum, with Warrick. Her fingers tightened on the cane, and she ran. But it was not the mindless trance it had been before. This was fear—fear, anger, and the unsettling desires of the magic inside her. Some magic, either Calum's or Warrick's, wanted its price, a sacrifice to pay its toll. Nim could not let Allister suffer for it. She could not let Warrick pay for what Calum had done.

She would find them. She would end this. There was not a moment to spare.

Guards turned at her footfalls. A weapon-wielding Maris behind her and Wes with his rod were surely suspect enough, but the accountants turned as well, their bearing clear and their intimations clearer: something was happening. Something they all had come to expect.

Something they'd been waiting for.

CHAPTER 12

Turning from the square to dodge as many of the king's guard as possible, Nim broke into her fastest run. Maris was faster but had not tried to stop the sprint at all, only fended off any who appeared to show an interest in interfering. Nim should have stopped. She knew she should because of the accountants—men and women of the Trust who traded magic for sacrifice and fed the power resting beneath the kingdom. They stood scattered along the alleyways and building fronts, and it was evident they were clearing the way for her. Their magic buzzed through her senses, tiny pushes and intimations to move citizen and guard alike. It did not touch Wesley, because Warrick's gift of sacrifice protected him, but the magic had not seemed to touch Maris either. It meant they were helping Nim, taking her where they wanted her to be.

She burst from an alley onto the roadway leading to the undercity with Maris and Wes. Nim was breathless and skittery. The lot of them had been propelled by more than simple fear. Nim's boots skidded to a stop on the cobblestone street, Wes stumbling to a standstill beside her, Maris elbowing her way in front of them both with a curse.

Maris being out front did nothing to protect Nim, because

before them, near the gates to the undercity and beneath a sun too low in the sky, was a scene that made Nim ill. It was horribly familiar—like a tableau of the painting she'd seen inside the king's room of locked cabinets. A painting brought to life. One of absolute conquest. Of subjugating one's enemy in the most theatrical way.

This, however, was no depiction of the head of the Trust being subdued. In place of the dark queen on the ancient canvas was Warrick, who had been brought to his knees. Calum stood before his brother, pride oozing from every part of his loathsome form. Nim wanted to end him. The cane pulsed in her hand, craving. It did not seem to care that it was Calum who had created it.

"Majesty," Maris warned just as Wes tugged on her sleeve to beg, "*Nim.*"

It was too late for her to run, even if she'd wanted to. From the distance, another voice called. *Ah*, it seemed to purr, *our lady queen.*

Calum's words were not spoken aloud, but Nim understood with painful clarity that they were meant for both her and the man at Calum's feet.

Warrick.

He did not look up at her, not that she expected him to hear his name in her head. Whatever gift they had to send her intimations, it did not work both ways. But she could feel that he knew she was there. She could feel that his emotions were tucked away. He did not need to tell her to run. Any fool would have known she should do that. Anyone who knew her at all would know that she could not.

She prepared to move, understanding that whatever action she took against Calum would be her last. Wes might protect her from magic, but she'd learned the hard way that Calum did not need magic to strike her down. None of that mattered. She only needed to get to Warrick. To free him.

As her boot rose, another figure burst from the alleyway, his run more agile than any cat or queen's protector. He had the sort of grace no amount of training could master. Nim did not take her eyes from the scene, but she felt Wes draw closer and Maris adjust her stance.

It was Rhen, come to find her. His magic didn't flare as strongly as Calum's, but his intimation was clearer, and Nim's stomach dropped, because the thought that he'd come for her had not been her own. Worse, Rhen had let slip that they were in more danger than she'd suspected.

She could see suddenly, through the thoughts that passed between Rhen and Calum, that the mass of shadow on the ground near the back of the tableau was not merely some discarded cloak. It was Allister, barely conscious, lying on the ground like refuse. He'd been no more than bait in a trap to draw Warrick in. It was just as Alice had feared—using Allister to snare a king had been Calum's plan all along. Because Nim cared about Allister. And Warrick cared about Nim. Once again, she had been his weakness. He'd been captured because of her.

Wes's grip on Nim's cape was all that made her hesitate from moving forward, from closing the distance that felt farther with every realization. She listened for Warrick, trying to sense what he might tell her, but there was only cold silence and Calum's preening. Nothing Warrick might say could go unheard by Calum and the accountants at their backs in any case, but it seemed as if something else held his words at bay.

"Majesty." Rhen's tone was as smooth as glass, entirely at odds with the intimation he hadn't meant for her to sense. He stopped beside them, Wes tucked neatly between a broken queen and a bastard prince, Maris out in front. Rhen took a breath then smoothed his vest into proper shape. "It seems I've caught you at an inopportune time."

She did not bother with a reply.

He sighed as if resigned to the fact that she would allow nothing but for them to face this fate. He looked at the scene before them, his older brothers and a scattered dozen of Calum's men, then back to her.

Rhen frowned then offered her his arm. "Shall we?"

Nim did not take the proffered arm. She adjusted her grip on the cane tucked against her. She moved swiftly, Wes beside her. Maris and Rhen kept near, noticeably leaving room to move. Their postures made clear the sort of outcome each expected—it would not end well.

They crossed the distance as a group. When she was near enough to recognize the blood soaking Warrick's shirt and the stillness in Allister's form, Nim felt her knees become weak. Rhen tensed beside her, but when he drew closer to offer support, her determination reared back. Warrick did not move, but his eyes rose, their emerald depths glowing unnaturally as he looked at her from beneath his brow. His hands were bound behind his back, knees on the stone. He might have appeared conquered, but there was no defeat in him. The glow in his gaze said he was enraged. His intimations were as silent as a grave.

"Brother," Rhen said to Calum, tone chiding. "Is the spectacle really necessary?"

Calum didn't spare him a look. "Miss Weston, so good of you to come. I wondered if you'd be clever enough to find us in time."

Warrick flinched, but whatever magic and chains bound him prevented him from acting. Besides, Calum loved that he was fighting. Warrick would be able to feel the joy radiating from Calum each time he tried, the same as Nim.

"Actually, she's a queen now," Rhen added conversationally. "I believe the title is *Majesty*."

Something hot shot through Calum's intimation as his gaze snapped to Rhen's. Out of the corner of her eyes, Nim could see Rhen's mouth widen in a playful smile, but she did not take her focus off Warrick. Seeing him bound sickened her, yet she could not look away.

"You seem cozy enough with your new queen," Calum said caustically.

Rhen's free hand went to his chest, his other still hovering near Nim's back. "You wound me, truly." In fact, it likely was true. The intimations from the watching Trust accountants seemed to be laughing right along with Calum, that Rhen was somehow more his father's son than his mother's.

They were taunting about Stewart, right there in front of Warrick on his knees. She wanted to murder them for it.

An abrupt shift in the onlookers cut short the thought. Every bit of attention was suddenly on Nim where she held Calum's cane. She didn't know if they could feel the magic or could understand what it craved, but it didn't exactly matter, as her intentions were made clear by the fact that she'd somehow come to be holding it before her, fingers gripped so tightly around it that they felt as if they might bleed.

She became aware, too, of Wes's grip on her cloak, tugging against her desire to move. On her other side, Rhen watched with some mixture of fascination and horror, but she could not parse which outcome he wanted more. The accountants stared raptly as well, their numbers slowly growing. They had come from dark corners and alleyways, drawn to the roiling power that called Nim herself forward—the meeting of Warrick's and Calum's magic, sons of the Trust together and their power at odds.

"Nimona." Calum's voice was calm and steady, but Nim had eyes only for Warrick.

His mouth had crawled into a one-sided grin at the sight of his brother's cane in his new bride's hands. The other side of his mouth had been busted, and there was a mark along his brow.

"What happens if I use it?" she asked.

"You will not." Calum moved closer to Warrick, flexing his magic as if in threat.

"Or what?" she asked Calum while her gaze remained on Warrick's. "What will you do if I no longer obey?"

"Nim," Wes croaked miserably behind her.

Warrick sent something warm and steady toward her, but Calum's magic seized tighter, and the feeling was gone. Her focus snapped to Calum.

"King Stewart is dead," she said coldly. "There is no threat of hanging. Who would you report my crime to?" She moved the cane into a more ready stance. It was long and built for a type of fighting she did not understand, but Nim had been using a mace for years. She knew how to hit well enough.

Calum's intimations were in check, but unease showed in his stare. He'd likely never considered anyone stealing his cane. After all, no one else could use a magic-forged weapon that was not their own.

"Who, I wonder, would pay the magic's toll?" She gave him a look. "Or has it already been paid?"

"If I may," Rhen started beside her, but she cut him off with a glare. He carefully inclined his head in acquiescence then shot Warrick an intimation that was a bit of a shrug.

"As it happens," Nim continued, "I've learned a thing or two of your laws."

One of the accountants slipped closer, and Maris shifted, the tilt of her blade making clear she had no compunctions about running him through. The intimations coming from the crowd made clear the accountants had no such compunctions either.

Nim's attention remained on Calum. "Warrick was made to pay for my use of his blade." The cane rolled slightly forward as she perfected her grip. "Which, if I'm not mistaken, would make you entirely responsible for whatever I do with this cane, by law." She glanced sideways. "Rhen?"

He cleared his throat then glanced at Calum. "It would seem so, yes."

"So go ahead," Nim told Calum. "Tell your mother."

"Lady Weston, you seem to have forgotten yourself entirely." Calum's voice was ice, but his intimation was colder. He sent an image of Warrick that was so horribly cruel and gruesome, she might have retched.

But anger propelled her forward. "Touch him one more time, and—"

Her words cut off as magic wrapped around her, a noose of power restricting her throat so she could barely breathe. Behind her, the sounds of Maris's blade and Wes's struggling revealed that he'd lost his hold on her, the only protection that could keep Trust magic at bay.

"Brother," Rhen said with a bit of steel. "You seem to have forgotten yourself as well. Do we no longer have manners? No shred of decorum?"

Calum's attention shot from Nim to Rhen, and Nim dropped to the ground as his magic was released. Whatever he'd opened his mouth to say, they would never hear because she waited not an instant before rolling to her feet in a move that closed the distance then released all she had with a single swing.

The cane cracked against Calum's leg, a good bit beneath the knee she'd aimed for, and an explosion of magic burst through the air. She had no idea if it was her strike or Calum's response, but Nim was knocked backward in a tumbling roll that ended several paces away. But her reaction to magic hadn't affected her the same way since she'd been bound to Warrick. She did not feel an impending swoon in the least. In fact, all she felt was the desire to bludgeon her victim again, to bleed him out on the stone street.

She was scrabbling toward him on the ground when someone grabbed her from behind, and she turned at the waist, cane raised to bash her attacker over the head.

"Nim!" Wes's shouts finally registered through the bleary, breathless haze, and she recognized it was him, gripping her leg for all he was worth as Maris fought off attackers behind them.

"Enough." Rhen's voice carried through the din in a manner that could only mean he'd done so with magic, and the lot of

Trust associates who fought Nim's protectors fell backward onto the ground. It was not unlike the way the courtiers had collapsed beneath Warrick's outburst in the throne room but somehow more silent and swift, more purposeful.

Panting, Nim looked away from the chaos to find Calum. He was a good distance apart from the group, getting to his feet—one foot, to be precise, as the one she'd struck lagged behind awkwardly—and his murderous intent focused solely on her.

She was going to kill him. She just needed to do one thing first. After flipping to her stomach, she crawled toward Warrick, who had not moved—could not move—from the pose in which he'd been bound. Wes scrabbled after, hanging onto her as if both their lives depended on it. And they absolutely did.

"Tell me," she pleaded. "Tell me what to do."

Warrick swallowed, staring down at her from a distance that somehow felt too far to cross. "It's too late. We must see this through now." His words from before came back to her: if ever he did not return, it would be only because he'd had no other choice. When he spoke again, his tone had changed, making clear he was speaking to someone over Nim's back. "Lay a hand on her, and your prize is forfeit."

Calum's intimation seemed to consider whether killing Nim might be worth the threat.

"He's right." Rhen's voice was steady, but Nim could not look away from Warrick's face.

He'd been beaten badly, but they had not hurt him in any permanent way. It had likely been only small wounds caused during their struggle to subdue him or a battle with Calum. What hurt worse was that the magic had him tied in ways that prevented him from sending intimations. He could not tell her what to do. He could not help her. But his gaze flicked to her bared head in a reminder that he had made her queen. He had given her power.

She took a slow breath, feeling Calum close in behind her.

Her fingers curled again around the cane. The pain in her knuckles disappeared entirely at the thought of what she was about to do. "No matter what comes," she said quietly to Warrick, "I will never regret choosing you." Then she turned and pressed to her feet.

CHAPTER 13

Calum's face was drained of color, his eyes as dark as onyx. He was heir to the Trust, and this close to the magic beneath the undercity, he was as strong as ever. Power crackled through the air, buzzing over Nim's skin, threatening to take her for its own, but she only cared about the sensation of the cane in her hand. Calum would answer for what he had done. The magic inside did not ask a single thing of her. Calum Lucus would pay its toll.

A sound like a wail came out of her as she lifted the weapon to strike again. Metal glinted, the first realization she had of the sword in Calum's hand, but she was not afraid. He raised the blade in an easy, graceful arc, and Maris's shouts rang through the crowd. Nim became aware quite suddenly of several different things. First, Maris was being held down by a dozen armed Trust men. Second, and more pressing, was that the tightness she felt around her middle was Wes, kneeling behind her, arms wrapped desperately about her waist.

Wes, who could not withstand a blade. Wes, who was the only thing protecting her from Calum's magic. She cursed when she understood that she'd doomed them both, and Calum grinned, his swing released a heartbeat before her own.

There was an explosion of power as the magic in his sword met the magic in the cane. Wes was knocked to the ground, screaming, and Nim was somehow locked within the grip of Calum's magic—or possibly that of the weapon in her hand. Her body felt as if it had lit on fire, every single part of her burning alive. Shouts echoed around them, but Nim could hear only the endless intimations Calum shoved through their bond: she would die with Warrick watching, Calum would paint the floor of his rooms with her blood. And more, something horrid, something that hurt in a way she could not comprehend. But she could not grasp her thoughts, could not quite keep hold of what was happening, only the deep desires of the cane and sword... then she felt a warning that slipped over her like a cool salve, a small reprieve from the fire.

Turn, it said. That was all.

The word made no sense, and yet she followed its command. Her body moved, twisting sideways, and Calum's blade slid down the cane with the force of his attack. For a frozen moment, anything at all might have happened. Then there was another push, another word, and Nim snapped back to herself, shot through with the panic and rage she'd lost before. She drove a fist across the space, hard into the place where Calum's chest met his throat. His sword slid again as he shoved back at her, and Nim shifted, the cane slipping so that his blade came up as she went down.

The cane clattered from her limp hand, and she rolled into Wesley on the street. He wrapped her into another desperate hug. He had to keep hands on her to save her from magic, but he could do nothing about the deadly sword. She couldn't seem to get control of her senses again and could not reach for the cane.

Calum raised his blade overhead. Then the world went still. The breath felt as if it had been sucked from Nim's lungs. The very air around her somehow no longer pressed on her skin. Calum's jacket hem, lifted by his movement, seemed to hover around him. The entire crowd and its chaos were suspended in the moment. The tingling, bitter tang of magic was on Nim's tongue, but it was not the cane or Calum's power.

It was worse. It was more. It was the thing that wanted to burn and to devour, to destroy what did not belong.

Her chest seized, and she jerked against Wesley's hold. His grip did not falter. Warrick made a sound, the only noise in all the madness, then Calum's sword clattered to the ground alongside his cane. Air returned to the street in a turbulent wind as the head of the Trust walked through the gates from the undercity.

She strode forward in a gown of liquid blackness, her dark hair still in the dying wind. Sensations slithered through the onlookers, none of them pleasant. Someone was meant to die. "Take him."

Nim should not have been able to picture the figure approaching or to understand that it was the head of the Trust—prostrate as she was on the ground—but she sensed the scene through the intimations of those around her. Their focus was too much, all at once, and her head throbbed. The head of the Trust had the ability to hide her approach—but she had not. She had wanted all to see.

Nim thought she might have lost a moment of time between the woman's command and her next breath, because when Nim opened her eyes again, the head of the Trust was standing before them. She looked mildly disgusted with the display as if she'd not been the one behind it in the first place.

Her order of *take him* had apparently been aimed at the Trust men who were gathering Calum to assist him back to the undercity. Several more of their men moved closer behind Warrick, who was still bound by Trust magic.

Warrick's mother gave him a long look before her gaze moved to Rhen, who shrugged.

"Do it," she said.

He pressed his lips together as if considering how to break

especially unpleasant news. Her response was less of an intimation and more of a warning. He sighed.

The head of the Trust turned to the waiting crowd. It seemed likely that most of the onlookers were Trust associates, as anyone in Inara with any sense would have hidden the moment they realized what was happening in their streets. But a few of Warrick's men, king's guard and kingdom watch, had stood by through the end.

"The kingdom is in turmoil, and yet its king has broken one of our oldest laws." Warrick's mother let her gaze trail over the onlookers, giving them her attention in what felt more like a threat than anything else. "My son and heir has betrayed the gravest of all laws. He has conspired to overthrow your queen: to collude against the Trust and its head." Her voice was a wicked blade, cleaving any hope for reprieve. "He will remain in Trust custody until he stands trial."

Nim's chest felt as if it were caving in, but it was not merely due to the pressure of magic. Calum's hold on Warrick had eased enough that a faint sense of his intimation came to her. *Go*, it said. *Go and do not come back.*

"No." Her voice was as faint as the intimation, but the head of the Trust stopped to stare down at her, still wrapped in Wes's arms.

"Perhaps you see now that you should not have fooled with forces you do not understand."

Nim coughed out a particularly unpleasant response, and the head of the Trust's gaze rose elegantly to her youngest son. *Rhen*, the gesture seemed to say, *you know what to do.*

Dipping his chin with slightly less than his usual grace, Rhen crossed the space, now scattered with the detritus of battle, to stand beside Warrick. They shared a look before Warrick's gaze returned to Nim.

Rhen lowered onto his haunches, close at Warrick's side, voice subdued. "Stewart was a good man."

Warrick's eyes did not move from Nim's. "He did not deserve what she has done."

She, he'd said. Their mother. The head of the Trust, not Rhen, had killed Stewart. Warrick was telling her, being certain she understood.

"It was never about Stewart. But you know that." Rhen's voice was uncharacteristically even. He reached behind Warrick then, to Nim's horror, removed the signet ring. Rhen stood, sliding the ring onto his own finger, with nary a word to the watching crowd.

Rhen had just made himself king. And with his elder brother in custody, all of it was legal.

Moontide, Warrick's intimation said. And Nim wanted to scream, *What? What happens at Moontide?* But Calum was moving again, free of the Trust men who'd tried to take him through the gates, and striding brokenly toward them—or, more specifically, toward Nim.

Rhen's gaze flicked to the head of the Trust, but she only watched as Calum made his way to Nim, plainly bloodthirsty and with ill intent.

"There are laws—" Rhen started, but Calum cut him off with a cruel blast of magic. One of the men near Warrick fell to his knees. Fates save him, the man must have been tied in a way that let him steal the sacrifice for Calum's magic. Allister still lay in a heap of dark fabric, and Maris was still held down by Calum's men.

Nim coughed, tasting blood, and Wes squeezed her ribcage tighter. They were going to die; she was sure of it.

Calum moved to stand over Nim, turning his head to give Warrick a telling glare. "Have no worries, brother. I will hold onto her for you."

"No," Rhen said, somewhat recovered from the hit and shifting to face Calum fully. The too-large signet ring turned on Rhen's finger as he pressed it with a thumb. "I'll be keeping her, thank you."

Rhen flicked a hand as if to order Wes and Nim scooped up like luggage, and the king's guard did just that. "This one too." He gestured, and the king's guard rounded the group to pick up Allister, whose arm flopped loosely away from his body when he was moved.

Nim scrambled to gain her footing before she could be hauled away, jerking free of one of the guards just as two more grabbed hold of her. "*No*," she shouted, her voice an anguished plea, but Warrick was sending her *go* again, *Go, go, go*.

"I *can't*," she told him.

"You have to," he said aloud, too calm, his eyes never leaving hers. *It's too late*, he reminded her. *We must see this through*.

"Warrick!"

"Go," Rhen told the guard. "Quickly." To Warrick, he inclined his head. "Brother." Then he took two steps forward and kicked the cane toward Calum. "And for you," he said affably with a glance at Calum's busted leg. "It seems you may need it after all."

CHAPTER 14

Nim was shoved into a carriage with Wes still clinging to her arm. He'd been hurt but apparently not so badly that it would take him down. Allister, who was unceremoniously wedged in beside them, had been hurt much worse. Wes appeared as if he might retch onto the carriage floor at any moment. Nim reached for Allister's hand but felt little response to her squeeze. She desperately needed to get them out of there.

Two guards waited at each door, but before she could even form a plan, a door opened. Rhen leapt in smoothly, giving a solid knock to the roof as he slid onto the bench seat opposite them, expression grim. The carriage lurched forward into what felt like a full run, juddering over the cobbled street, away from the Trust. Away from Warrick.

Fury rose through Nim again. "You filthy—"

Rhen held up a finger, and she launched from Wes's grip before Wes had hold of her again, dragging them awkwardly back on the seat beside Allister.

"Nim," he begged against her shoulder, "let him take us back. Let him get us to the castle." He sounded as miserable as she

93

felt. They'd never had a chance to save anyone. Calum had only wanted her to see, to flaunt his trophy. To be sure Warrick saw, so that both he and Nim understood how thoroughly Calum had won. Somehow, horribly, Nim had lost Warrick before she'd even known he was at risk.

"He's your *brother*," Nim hissed to Rhen. "The *king*. How can you leave him like that? You think you are safe now, happy to wear Stewart's ring. But one day, you'll be at a disadvantage," she promised. "And I will be there to toss you into the pit." Even if she had to rise from her own grave to do it, she would.

Rhen frowned. "I was hoping you'd be a bit less murderous without the cane."

She jerked forward again, but Wes was stronger, and she fell back into a feeble heap of limbs. Then, because she could not seem to help it, she screamed. All it earned her was less energy to draw herself breath and a wince from Rhen. Allister hadn't moved at all.

"Majesty," Rhen said with deference, "we both know it was Warrick's wish that you be returned to the castle before you found yourself in more trouble than"—he gestured vaguely— "well, this."

Nim's voice was hoarse; everything about her felt raw. "And what of the trouble *he* is in?"

"She will not harm Warrick before the trial."

A weak whimper escaped Nim. *Before the trial.* She felt sick. Heartbroken. The Trust was taking Warrick underground, and he might never come back out. She felt as wretched as ever, but strangely, not at all like she needed Allister's salts. In fact, if she wanted for anything, it was for the return of the weapon's power in her hand.

Her head spun. The day had started as a mission for rescue. And she *was* feeling murderous. She hated Calum and his vile cane. They were out of her reach, and Warrick was at the mercy of both the man and his weapon.

"How did this happen?" she groaned, dropping her head back to stare at the ceiling. She didn't understand the magic's hold on her or how it had bound Warrick.

Rhen sighed. "I'm afraid, my lady queen, explanations will have to wait until we've returned to the safety of the castle."

The carriage jolted. Clamoring sounded outside, followed by the broken clatter of unsteady hoofbeats then the unmistakable peal of swords and screams of men.

They had returned to the castle, but the king's guard were earning their wages completing the task. By the time Nim and Wesley were safely ensconced in Nim's old suite, half the men were limping, ragged, and in need of assistance of their own. Rhen had followed closely, barking commands at every turn. He might have used his magic more often, but the threat was coming not from Trust associates but Inara's own—citizens who had no magic and who feared it. And, she suspected, Rhen's fighting with Calum had done more damage than he intended to let on.

"There," Rhen said, gesturing the guards carrying Allister through the sitting room door toward the bed in which Nim had once slept. "Bring him the king's physician and food and drink. Something light and—" He glanced at the staggered faces of the men and women gathered in Nim's sitting room. "Send up tea for everyone, fresh water to wash, and clothes. Then change out the guard and get Garrett in to the second physician. That arm does not look well."

Nim hadn't meant to react, but Rhen saw her surprise that he knew the guard's name, let alone had paid mind to his wounds. Rhen's mouth shifted in something of a tell, but whatever the regret was, he didn't voice it. "You," he said, pointing to Nim, "sit."

She did, if for no other reason than she was exhausted, and Wesley collapsed in a heap beside her, finally letting go of his grip.

Allister had come to for what felt like only a heartbeat of time in the corridor, and the men who'd brought him in had handed him over to Bramwell and another guard. Bramwell had promised that Allister would be fine, saying he'd seen it before. That promise had meant more than all the reassurance Rhen had tried to give before it.

"Alice," Nim said, coming to her feet.

Rhen gave her a look that commanded her to sit down again, but before he could order anyone else to look into it, Maris spoke up. She'd been bloodied a bit during her own struggles with the Trust men and had tied a strip of cloth about her forearm. Maris was a trained protector, though, and had taken the hits well, as well as being prepared with proper armor.

"I'll fetch her," Maris said. "Send one of the guards, and she's liable to club them with a candlestick."

Rhen gave her a look that seemed to question what was with high ladies using candlesticks as weapons, but he did not ask.

Bramwell returned to the main suite and bowed his head to Nim, hand on his sword with clear intention he meant to use it, to go after Warrick with a contingent of men. "With your permission—"

"No," Rhen said. "No one makes an attempt on the undercity without my command."

The guard's dark eyes snapped to his.

Rhen gave the man his full attention. It was quite disconcerting, even from where Nim sat. "I understand where your loyalties lie," he said calmly. "But your duty now is to your queen."

Bramwell's look of utter betrayal swept the room, landing on Maris last.

"It's true," she told him. "I saw with my own eyes. This is the path Warrick wants us to follow." Maris gave Rhen a considering glance. "And while I may never bow to another king, I stand by our lady queen. Until the end." Her sigh seemed to acknowledge that it might not be long at all. "Majesty." Giving a cursory bow, she said, "I shall return with Alice posthaste."

Beside Nim, Wes fell backward onto the couch with a sigh of his own.

"Curse it," Nim said. "Bramwell, please fetch Margery. She'll be worried sick."

"Ah." The word had come from Rhen in such an unnatural tone that the remaining guard, Nim, and Wes all turned to look at him.

He winced.

Nim stood.

"I... have her."

"What do you mean you *have* her? Where is Margery? What have you done?"

Nim's words cut like a blade, and Rhen's answering intimation said he felt it as sharply as she intended. "My lady—"

"Queen." She stalked closer, rage building once more in limbs she'd thought would be useless with exhaustion for weeks. Before she realized precisely what she was doing, her finger was jabbing into his chest, punctuating every word. "My. Lady. Queen."

"Nim," Wes hissed behind her, doing his level best to put some energy of his own into the grip he had on her.

Rhen had not retreated under the attack but still radiated chagrin. "I assure you it was never my intent—"

"Where is she?"

He winced harder. "Perhaps it's best that I collect her now and we argue on it later."

Nim crossed her arms. "If you think I'm leaving you alone for one moment to trot around this castle, pretending to be king—"

His expression changed, and her anger flared hotter.

"Bramwell," she ordered, not taking her eyes off Rhen. "Fetch my sword."

Wes groaned.

Rhen rolled his eyes. "Stay your hand, Bramwell. We shall fetch Margery, not our swords." He gave Nim a look. "Then I suggest our lady queen take a nap."

Nim swung, but Wes caught her arm, throwing them both off balance.

"Come," Rhen said. "She's liable to be just as spirited as you by now."

CHAPTER 15

Nim suspected Margery would be a good deal more than spirited. If she knew her friend at all, Margery would be saving her energy for the first person to open the door.

For her part, Nim was livid. "You locked her in a *tomb*?"

"It's a vault room. There's not a single body in there with her. And she has candles and water."

"For all that is sacred," Wesley whispered beside them. "She's going to murder you."

Rhen raised his gaze to the ceiling as he unlocked the door, as if fate might swoop down and save him from the entire ordeal. It would not. And whatever happened, he had it coming.

The lock clicked, and Rhen cautiously pushed in the heavy door.

Inside, the room was dark. Light from the torches in the corridor cast flickering shadows over papers strewn across the ancient vault floor. There were thin bits of metal broken and scattered near the entrance, as if Margery had tried picking the lock. The vault was silent.

"Maybe she found another way out." Wes's voice was small, wary.

"There is no other way out." Rhen glanced at Nim then took a torch from the wall and started inside.

There was a very loud *crack* when the iron candlestick came down on his head. The torch rolled to the floor, and Rhen stumbled forward. From the darkness, Margery came for him again, weapon raised for another hit.

Nim reached out to stop her, but she couldn't quite decide if helping Rhen was the thing to do. She considered, for a flash, dragging Margery out and slamming the vault door behind them, but Rhen had apparently not been fool enough to leave the key in the lock. Besides, he had magic. They'd have to actually kill him if they didn't want him to escape.

Wes stared, apparently also unsure if or how to act. Bramwell only smiled. Before anyone might have even had time to react, though, Rhen spun, grabbed the candlestick to yank Margery closer, then seized hold of her wrist. He had her disarmed and pinned against him in less than a breath. Her face was set to vengeance, but he did not seem to be hurting her. Behind them, the torch flickered out, not a single of the king's documents caught by flame.

Nim stepped forward. "Margery, are you well?"

She blinked.

Nim pressed her lips together. "Right. Let's get you out of here."

A woman approached from the other room, stack of parchment in hand, and stared at the group of stragglers in the narrow space outside the king's vault. She seemed to recognize one was the queen and fell into a deep curtsy. "Majesty."

"Oh," Nim answered, "Lady Pehn. We'll be out of your way momentarily. I apologize for the..." Nim gestured toward the vault, decided against saying *desecration*, then cleared her throat. "Thank you for your assistance earlier. I'm grateful to have such a loyal, trustworthy magistrate in place."

At the word *magistrate*, Margery leaned forward in Rhen's

hold to peer out the doorway, took in the woman in the proper black gown and the robes of her office, and let loose a cry of rage the likes Nim hadn't heard since... well, at least since she'd done so herself earlier the same day.

"Not to put too fine a point on the matter," Rhen said once they'd returned to Nim's rooms. "I never told you I was the magistrate. It was entirely an assumption on your part."

"I will tell you precisely where you can shelve your assumptions—" Margery started, leaning toward him with a clear indication that she did not mean to wait.

Nim placed a hand on Margery's arm. "While I can appreciate your absolutely righteous anger in this matter, I'm afraid we need to put it away for just a moment until we can sort—"

"I'm afraid he needs sorted now," Margery argued, apparently choosing to ignore the disconcerting look Rhen gave that said he might be interested in taking her on. She turned to Nim. "If you think I am willing to work with him after what he's done, you have lost all grip of sense."

"All that was *done* was that you were kept from harm for the few short hours—" Rhen tried before a tea kettle was launched at his head.

"You killed King Stewart," Margery raged.

"Did I?"

Nim pursed her lips. Warrick had all but announced to the watching crowd that their mother had been the one to end the king. He'd wanted Nim to understand that for some reason. She wasn't in any particular hurry to help Rhen, though.

Margery's fists slammed to her sides. "You kidnapped Nim and dragged her into the undercity."

Rhen winced. "That, I did. But, to be fair, she stabbed me in return. I believe that would make us square."

Margery's eyes narrowed. "She. Was. Stabbed. Back."

"Yes, but not by me."

Nim pressed her fingers to the bridge of her nose. "Margery, we must consider this. We've no other choice." She loosed a heavy breath then glanced at the door to be certain it was closed.

Bramwell stood guard, his eyes on Maris across the room, where she stitched a wound on her own arm after refusing help from the others.

Alice, wedged between Nim and the space Margery had been taking up for the performing of violent maneuvers, said, "I'm with Margery."

Rhen frowned. "The subject is not open to voting. Our lady queen is right. There's no other choice." He met Nim's gaze. "For any of us."

Whatever he meant to convey to her, she was not picking up. There was no telling whether it was exhaustion or something else. "Alice," Nim said after a moment, "please go check on Allister." She touched a hand to the girl's head. "And close the door behind you."

Alice nodded, giving not even a glance back, and the room fell silent until the door snicked closed.

Nim faced Margery. "The Trust has taken Warrick."

Margery looked suddenly quite ill.

"So," Nim said, "as loathe as I am to even consider it, we've no one else but Rhen." A bit of the heat came back to Margery's cheeks, but the fight had gone out of her. "Besides, I believe this is what Warrick wishes, even if I've no idea why." Margery's gaze rose to hers, and Nim explained, "He was bound somehow, and I was unable to sense whatever he meant to tell me."

Margery sank to the sofa, a long, delicate hand coming to rest over her heart.

Rhen let the silence sit for a moment as the horrible truth settled over Margery, then he took a step closer to Nim.

"I need answers," she said.

"Of course."

"Warrick may have confirmed that you did not kill Stewart,

but you are not free of guilt. You taunted. You played. You helped her." She did not say, "He was your father," because Stewart had never even known he'd sired a second son. The head of the Trust had kept Rhen's parentage hidden, and not just from the king.

"Yes."

Nim crossed her arms.

He cleared his throat. "This would all be a great deal less complicated, you understand, if not for such..."

She raised a brow as he apparently struggled.

He offered her a half smile in return. "There are certain restrictions put on someone so close to... to someone of great power." He shrugged, seemingly uncomfortable. "If you take my meaning."

Nim did take his meaning. She understood all too well. "Warrick was bound not to speak of her or, in fact, of you." He watched her. "And yet," she said, "it seems you're able to send intimations so clearly, it's as if you're in my thoughts."

"Mmm," he said, but not in the pleasant, noncommittal way Warrick always had. "Powerful magics can be very difficult to navigate."

"Helpful," Margery muttered from the couch.

Rhen closed his eyes for a long moment. "I've told you before that I am not bound in the same exacting way as some of the others. It does not mean I'm free to..." His voice trailed off, and when Rhen's eyes opened again, Nim felt him become aware that she was staring at the stockinged toes peeking out beneath Margery's skirts.

So many bindings placed on my brothers, he had said. *Rules upon rules*. Nim's eyes rose to his.

"Indeed," he said, apropos of nothing. He slid a hand casually into his pocket. "I should leave you both to rest."

"What?" Nim's voice was sharper than she intended, and Wesley popped up to sitting from where he'd been dozing behind the couch, hair askew and eyes bleary. Nim glared at

Rhen. "You can't leave without answering the rest of our questions. How are we meant to get Warrick? Moontide is in a matter of days. What are we supposed to do?"

Rhen inclined his head, his intimation chiding. It said he'd given her the only answer he could, and she'd said she understood.

"You can't tell me? That's your answer?" She shook her head, too tired to helm the rage that flowed through her. "Someone get my dagger."

There was something sad in the smile he attempted. "I'm afraid that will not help you. In fact, I suspect using Warrick's magic while he's kept away from you will only cause him pain."

She scowled.

"I've given you what I can for now," Rhen said. "But word will have spread about Warrick's capture, and Inara's queen will need to speak to its citizens. Rest. Rest and eat, and I'll be back for you soon." *We have a kingdom to hold together.*

Cold dread sank into Nim's gut as Rhen walked past, but she could not parse whether it was hers or his. When he reached the door, he glanced over his shoulder at her. "The whole thing would have been less complicated before you came along." *Now,* his intimation said, *it's too late to do anything but see it through.*

Nim sank onto the couch beside Margery as the door closed behind Rhen. Wes gave her shoulder a pat before he returned to his pillows on the floor.

"I abhor that man," Margery muttered.

"As do we all." Nim could not help but think of his words, though, and the events on the day of Stewart's death. It was true that Rhen had let Stewart believe Warrick had betrayed him. But Rhen had never known the man as a father, only as one who'd tried repeatedly to bring down the Trust.

Furious that Rhen had taken Stewart's faith in him as the king lay dying, Warrick had sent a very clear intimation that Rhen should run. Rhen had only shaken his head and said, "No, brother, it's far too late for that."

Far too late. Again and again.

Stewart had died beneath Warrick's hand that day, and Warrick had been devastated by the loss. Warrick's intimations had been unreserved as he stood over Rhen—that the Trust had driven them to that moment. Nim recalled his thoughts that the queen had meant to take the kingdom, to free herself from the binds of the undercity and rise unchallenged, to devour the kingdom. She would steal from it sacrifices until there was nothing left and she ruled all beneath stone and below sky.

Nim had not understood. Warrick had blamed their mother all along, not Rhen, who'd only been a pawn in her game. A pawn like Nim. And Rhen had said that she was clever. Clever like him.

She took Margery's hand in hers. "Rhen pushed Warrick to take the throne. If he'd wanted to steal it, he might have done so right then, when Warrick was distracted. He didn't."

In fact, Warrick had sent Rhen away with a warning for their mother: *Go to her and tell her what she has done. This blood is on her hands, and I will repay her in kind. She will suffer until she prays for her own end. Tell her that is my vow.*

"Warrick gave me a choice that day: to leave or stand by him. Save myself or surrender to whatever was about to be done. I chose Warrick, knowing full well he intended to go to war with the Trust. I can't run from it now. If he wants me to ally with Rhen, I will." She glanced at her friend. "But you do not have to."

"I'm offended that you would say such a thing."

Nim sighed. "And yet you know I must."

"It's a mess," Margery agreed. "But I could never leave you to face it alone, even with that dastardly spawn of crooked fate with his vile grin and serpent's tongue." At Nim's look, Margery only shrugged. "I had some time to think on insults locked in that vault. It's not as if there was anything of use in the documents. Certainly if there was a contract of any sort, it was hidden elsewhere, or someone got to it before us. I suspect the good-for-nothing scoundrel knew so all along. Elsewise, he'd never have let me in, let alone helped dig through parchments for hours. Like he didn't have a care in the world."

"Margery," Nim said after a long moment, "what, precisely, happened in that vault that you came away with no shoes?"

CHAPTER 16

Nim stood as queen before a council of courtiers and agents of the kingdom, Warrick's brother, third in line as heir to the Trust and somehow also acting king of Inara, at her side. She felt as if she might be sick. Beside her, opposite Rhen, stood Wes and a heavily armed Maris. Bramwell and several of Warrick's personal guard were scattered about the room, gazes alert in a less-than-comforting reminder that all of Inara wanted the queen and her accomplices dead. Particularly determined, it seemed, were the courtiers and agents of the king.

"We stand before you as sovereigns, eager to work with each of you to put the turmoil of the past days to rest," Rhen said evenly. "But make no mistake, one move against your queen or her supporters, and you will answer to me."

His magic swam over Nim's senses, stinging and biting like the scar that marked her shoulder in sacrifice to magic. She did not know if the others felt his power in the way she had, but they shifted uncomfortably, clearly understanding the threat.

Lady Constance, Lady Pehn, and Lady Lora stood together on one side of the gathered crowd, Lady Sybil on the other. Margery, dressed in a clean gown and borrowed boots, stood near the center a few bodies deep, her gaze on a group of men

Nim did not recognize. They were fairly young, heavily armed, and noticeably situated around a blond man with a narrow face.

"Majesty," Rhen said, apparently handing the grim duty of addressing their situation over to Nim.

Her attention snapped back—to the very thing she'd been working so hard not to focus on. Warrick was gone. He'd been taken into the undercity, and she did not know if they could get him back. He was meant to be king, but he did not matter only to the future of Inara. He mattered to Nim. He mattered every moment, every heartbeat, and every instant she had left.

The courtiers watched her, waiting, and she realized she did not care if they wanted her hanged. Her duty as queen was clear. She was meant to lead, to decide. Before her were the men and women responsible for the protection of the kingdom. At the very least, she had to tell them what had happened. She didn't know if she could do it.

This is where he wants you, Rhen's intimation said. Nim realized he'd barely sent intimations to her at all, as if he were being careful to stay out of her head.

Leading Inara had become her duty, certainly, but nothing aside from the reminder of Warrick's wishes might have given her the strength to do what he had asked of her. Shoulders straight, she said, "Inara's king has been taken by the Trust."

A shocked outcry rocked the crowd, unsurprising despite that they had wanted Warrick killed. Nim had just revealed that their biggest fears were continuing to come true. More, they were about to discover that the man standing beside her had named himself king, however temporarily. If they wanted Warrick—whom they'd known well and had once held great respect for—hanged, then Rhen might be the worst they could fathom.

The poor souls had no idea.

"He will face trial come Moontide, by judgment of the Trust." She let her gaze roam the crowd, a reminder that their responses were being observed. "Until that day, Stewart's second heir will stand in his place at my side, to keep Inara secure until the rightful king is returned."

Someone in the crowd shouted for Rhen's head, and several more drew swords. There was a scuffle in the back, which the guard quickly brought to order. A knife hurled at the dais barely missed Rhen as he edged Nim a few steps out of the way.

Well, this is going better than I expected, he thought at her. *The first blade missed.*

She blew out a breath, prepared to launch into a series of shouted arguments with agents of the kingdom at the very least, but the blond man in the crowd stepped forward.

Before he could speak, Rhen's voice rang like a warning. "Lord Avery Preston."

The agitated crowd stilled, eyes on Rhen and the man who had moved. Preston had Trust blood, and Calum had put him in place should Warrick and Rhen not take Stewart's throne. He stared on, the very man Nim and her friends had been trying to find when Rhen had accosted her at the king's ball.

She couldn't sense magic from Preston, but the way his hand rested on the hilt of his sword spoke clearly enough. He had no fear of Rhen and no fear of the room. The man held power, and it showed in the easy confidence he exuded.

Beside her, Maris shifted, ready with her own sword.

"So good of you to come," Rhen said to the man as if dismissing him out of hand.

Rhen's intimations had closed off entirely once more, and Nim could not help but wonder exactly how much freedom the head of the Trust had given her youngest son. Rhen's jaw flexed infinitesimally as Margery shifted behind the group that included Preston and his associates.

"Carry on, Your Majesty." Rhen's hands stayed still at his sides, his gaze focused just to the side of the man staring back at him.

"I understand that the past days have been trying. In that, none of us are alone. But the threat posed to the kingdom is too great not to stand together. I ask that you put aside your reservations regarding our king until the true danger is behind us."

"You are correct, Lady Weston," a man near Lord Preston said coolly. "The threat posed to the kingdom is great indeed. And surely such peril should only be faced by a true king of Inara."

Shouts and murmurs of approval rumbled through the crowd before the crack of Rhen's voice returned the room to silence. "I warned you once. I will not do so again."

The man who'd spoken moved forward under a power not his own, seemingly dragged across the floor with his feet trailing behind him, to stop before the crowd, where he was dropped onto his hands and knees. "Our lady queen will receive the respect she deserves."

The man did not look up, though it was evident his bow was not in deference. In the watching crowd, Lord Preston stared on, his golden eyes pinned on Rhen.

I am king, Rhen's stance seemed to reply. *I shall have my games.*

It was such an odd thought, entirely out of place, and yet Nim thought she had begun to understand. Rhen had said he was tied but not in the same manner as his brothers. Lord Preston might not rank higher than heir to the Trust or a king on a throne, but he had Rhen's mother at his back. He was another piece in her game.

After Rhen had knocked the serpent meant for Nim from her desk, he had said his best move was to stay on the gameboard. He'd said there was a power play in the Trust, treachery and secrets about. She had paid no mind to him then, but that was before Warrick had urged her to leave with Rhen.

Secrets and bound things. She wanted to ask him what would happen if she shined light on those secrets—if she found a way to destroy the protections that kept Warrick and Rhen from acting. But Nim knew the answer rested beneath the foundations of Inara. The kingdom had not simply been built over the

Trust. Their histories were woven together, and somehow, after Stewart had made his bargain, so were their fates.

The unrest had worsened as Nim's thoughts circled darkly, and the crowd had inched closer to the dais where Nim stood as queen.

"Enough," snapped someone in the crowd, and several courtiers again traded blows.

"Lady Sybil, if you please," Nim said.

The woman inclined her head with a gratified tilt to her lips then issued a sharp command as a half dozen of her guard struck the fighting courtiers before clamping them into irons. She made quick work of the crowd, taking one of the men near Lord Preston herself in something that felt of wicked pleasure. When the man was on his knees before Preston and his lot, Lady Sybil's gaze shifted to Rhen.

Nim could not read whatever passed from their new seneschal to their new king, but she had not forgotten their confrontation in Sybil's office. The look Rhen gave now made clear that he was no longer a station below her. In fact, it seemed to promise that he did not intend to execute his new position gracefully.

Lady Sybil did not seem surprised. Her task complete, she inclined her head once more to Nim.

"I ask again," Nim said, "that we stand together. As such, we've assembled a plan of action." Her next words were directed at Lord Preston. "But I vow to you now, any who are discovered not to have followed these commands to the letter will be hanged on the square."

CHAPTER 17

"Well done," Rhen said, giving Nim an appreciative nod that made her feel strangely satisfied.

She splashed her hands in a basin of water, glad that no one had seemed to notice that they'd been sweat slicked and trembling. "How many more like Preston are out there?"

More, certainly, and maybe more like Lady Sybil, who was on Warrick's side.

Rhen glanced at the few watching guard. Most of the others had gathered with Margery and Wes to discuss the details of Nim's commands. "Perhaps we should speak of it somewhere more private. Are you up for a walk?"

A huff of air escaped Nim as she dried her hands. She felt as if she might collapse, but that was not the sort of thing a queen was meant to do. "Yes."

Rhen gave her a look, but as Margery approached, his expression slid back to its idle state.

"Preston will never do as you've commanded," Margery told Nim. "But should he manage somehow to get out of it, Lady Constance and I have located a record of his coin. The man is as good as handled."

"Thank you," Nim said. "I could do with one less concern at the moment."

"What next?"

Nim glanced at Rhen. "We're going for a stroll, apparently."

"Somewhere pleasant, I presume." Margery's tone was cutting.

Rhen ran a hand over his vest, but the added layer of king's robes made the gesture awkward. "The dungeons, in fact. You are very welcome not to come if you'd prefer."

Margery hooked her arm into Nim's. The corner of Rhen's mouth twitched in something that was not a smile.

Wes, Margery, Bramwell, and two other trusted guards accompanied them through the castle, deeper and deeper down twisting stairwells and dimly lit corridors to what was, indeed, a dungeon-like tomb. Rhen led the group forward, his magic lighting the ancient torches in the cavernous space with a too-steady, unflickering flame.

Senses swimming, Nim took in the room. A line of cells was carved into one wall, metal brackets cemented into another. It was cool but dry, and the floors were dusted with small bits of stone and mortar, as if the walls, or possibly the vaulted ceilings, had shed. Nim did not like it at all.

"What are you about?" Maris asked from behind them.

"My lady," Rhen said. "While you may not recognize me as king, surely you can manage the dignity due, say, a lowly lord?"

Maris watched him with narrowed eyes.

"Right. As expected." He turned back to the blank wall opposite them, seeming to orientate himself, then swept a foot across the floor. "Bramwell, sword."

Bramwell approached cautiously but held the weapon forward. Rhen took it with practiced ease, tossed it handle first so that he might grab the blade, then knocked the hilt into the floor in one fluid movement.

Beneath the pommel, the earth and stone gave way, falling

into darkness. Nim and the others stepped back. Rhen only turned. *Hmm*, his gesture seemed to say. *Would you look at that.*

From the hole came a dark sensation, tempting Nim nearer. It called to her in the way that the magic beneath the undercity did, with false promises, lulling her closer when some part of her knew it was meant to devour. She felt Rhen's arm cross her body to block her from moving closer, startling her back to her senses before she'd even realized she'd moved. His dark eyes met hers.

Another secret, another thing he'd been bound from telling her. But Rhen had not told her at all. Indeed, he'd acted as if she'd just happened upon it.

She nodded assurance that she had herself under control, and he dropped his arm, but he did not take his attention from her. There was clearly something he needed her to see, to understand. A pit. Right there in the castle, beneath the kings and queens gone past.

"What is that?" Bramwell asked.

"Their power," Nim whispered. "The same as beneath the Trust."

"Inside the castle?" Bramwell had known about Warrick, but by the sound of things, having a river of magic beneath his feet was too much to fathom.

Rhen's answer was quiet, his attention still on Nim. "Secrets have always been inside the castle." He glanced over Nim's shoulder, at the cells along the wall. "Why else would it need so many passages?"

It seemed as if something pained him, and his gaze snapped away from the wall. He took a breath, gestured Nim to move backward, then stepped away from the pit.

"Cover it," Margery said.

Bramwell found a grate near the wall and placed it over the floor, though Nim knew well enough the true danger was not someone happening upon it and falling in.

"We can go," she told Rhen, sensing he needed to get away from what he had revealed.

He nodded then led them out through the single door they'd come in. But Rhen did not turn up the narrow stair outside and instead headed down another darkened corridor. Wes pulled one of the magic-fueled torches from the wall and stayed close to Nim. The steady flame of the light threw shadows at strange angles. Maris's sword remained drawn.

When they passed a crossing corridor, the familiarity of it made Nim hesitate. Apparently hearing her step falter, Rhen glanced back at her. His eyes were pinched, expression guarded. Nim stopped, and Rhen turned, giving a nod that she go ahead if it pleased her.

Rather than bothering to glare at him for sending the intimation instead of just speaking, she only turned, Wes at her side, and followed the vague memory that tugged at her.

"I've been here." Wes's voice was quiet, as if the sound might awaken something none of them wanted to see.

"I believe I have as well," Nim said. "Though I'm not certain which direction..."

Wes held the torch higher, and the shape of another doorway came into view. They both moved toward it.

Margery and Maris were quiet behind them, but Nim could tell they did not like the idea of exploring the catacombs and corridors beneath Inara Castle. Nim couldn't have stopped herself if she'd wanted to. Something stronger than the pull of magic was calling to her. Memories of a child who dearly loved her father. A child who had not yet been touched by magic.

"There." At the end of the corridor was another, lit by thin shafts of light coming from somewhere above. The group followed, Rhen at the rear. Wes and Nim took them into a more polished gallery, a narrow room with fine cut stones, the walls hung with massive pieces of art. Large fabric sheets, the material dingy and aged, covered many of them. Wes paused as if caught in a memory, his gaze trailing over the room.

Nim moved toward a large painting at random and tugged the drapery to fall at her feet. She stepped back to look up at it, a scene of the kingdom that rose more than three men tall. "I've seen this before," she said as Margery came to stand beside her. "With my father."

Margery's hand slid into Nim's. She said not a word.

Wes's torch tilted toward a relief sculpture of a man with a sword, one hand tangled in the reins of a massive rearing horse.

Rhen came to Nim's other side, and his magic lit the dozen torches lining the room.

"How many more does she have in the castle?" Nim asked. How many Trust men and women had infiltrated Inara, she meant. How many of their kind did the head of the Trust have in place.

"More than you can count."

"I am fairly good with numbers," Nim said.

His silence seemed to reply that he understood.

"Have we any chance?"

Rhen's gaze trailed over the painting. The kingdom had been depicted in such a manner that implied it was nothing more than a majestic realm of kings and their court, grand and imposing, as if no darkness hid below. "I cannot answer that."

"And who else like Lady Sybil?" Who was on their side?

He looked at her then, his mouth gone devious. "You might be surprised."

Margery's sigh said she was done with his evasiveness. Then she just said so right out.

"They're all watching you," Nim said to Rhen. "Both the Trust associates and Warrick's allies."

"And what a sight I am to see."

She held his gaze. He certainly was a sight to see. He certainly was *something* indeed.

"The Trust has stolen family from each of us." Nim's words were even, not an accusation nor question. She wasn't sure what it was exactly she wanted him to reply, only that she needed to say it, to remind Rhen he was their enemy, no matter that they may be momentarily on the same side.

"Yes," Rhen said, just as evenly. "Each of our fathers as well."

Something snaked over Nim, but it was not the sense of magic. It was a truth, cold and horrible, that said Rhen's mother would destroy anyone at all who got in her way. He believed Warrick was safe, but only until it no longer served their mother's plans.

Rhen had once assured Nim that he had motivations of his own, that he did not pander to the whim and will of his brother, heir or no. She had mistaken his intent at the time. She would not mistake him again.

"Lady Margery," Nim said without turning from Rhen, "I think it's time we retired to my room."

CHAPTER 18

Nim sat perched on the edge of Allister's bed, where he'd been propped on a half dozen pillows by Margery and Wes. She held one of his hands in hers; his other hand rested carefully over his stomach. His dark hair had been sorted perfectly into its place as if he'd not just had a run in with the Trust. Alice lay curled up on the foot of the bed, evidently having worn herself thin caring for him since his return.

"How badly does it hurt?" Nim asked Allister.

"Not at all."

Nim smiled softly at him. Across the room, settled amicably before a nearly empty plate of cakes, Wes and Margery talked in hushed tones.

"I've managed quite a mess for us all, haven't I?"

Allister drew a steady breath. "It was never your mess, was it, Majesty?"

"Please don't call me that." She squeezed his hand. "It's a mess, and we're in it, and here I sit, beneath an impotent crown." Her eyes met his. "What good is being queen without Inara?" Without Warrick. Without a shred of safety for her friends. "You do not deserve this, none of you."

"Inara will stand, despite the magic. It has stood since time beyond record. Whatever comes, this will still be the kingdom we love, whether we deserve it or no."

"Will it?" Nim asked. "If the kingdom was so strong, then why would Stewart have made a bargain with the head of the Trust? Why trade peace for his own heirs? He must have known, surely, that there was no hope to defeat what was coming."

"Fear," Allister said. "And fear is not something owned by Inara alone."

"What do you mean?"

His hand, still on the blanket, tensed in a way that must have been caused by pain. He was trying so hard not to let her see it that she decided not to mention it. She would ask the doctor to check on him again just to be certain. "Calum made a bargain," Allister explained. "He traded his freedom to move about the kingdom in exchange for keeping Warrick from the Trust."

She stared back at him. Allister was entirely right. Calum had given up so much. She'd never discovered why.

"All we face teaches us in the end." Allister's dark eyes were steady on hers. "So, my lady queen, what have we learned?"

NIM CURSED HERSELF AS A FOOL. Time and again, Warrick and Rhen had tried to show her. She'd been so distracted by Calum's games and the threat of the Trust that she hadn't seen that they all had something to lose, not just Nim and Warrick.

Glancing over her shoulder to be certain she was alone, she slipped into another passageway, one that brought her closer to the king's hidden room. The keys she'd found in Warrick's desk slid right into the lock despite how complicated the mechanism looked, and the door snapped open beneath her hand.

She stood in the center of King Stewart's silver room, taking in the space with new eyes. Nim had no way of knowing whether fear had driven Stewart, but she was certain it was not what had driven his men. His advisors had sacrificed everything to save Inara. They had placed all their hopes into one outcome, into the fate of one man. Not Stewart but Warrick. The head of the Trust's son.

Wes might not be able to recall his parents because he'd been so young, but Nim remembered hers. She had known her father with all of her being, understood his loyalty to the kingdom to the pit of her soul. He had believed she could do this. He'd believed, at the very least, that it could be done.

Nim crossed the space to the painting she'd seen over Warrick's shoulder, then she tore loose the drapery covering it. The cloth was not dusty or scented with age, unlike the rest of the room, which seemed as if it had been abandoned to time. She stared up at the scene, somehow drawn to touch it. Her fingers hovered over figures painted in an unlikely pattern of broad strokes and fine detail.

"What are you hiding?" she whispered, gaze trailing over the lines of a long-ago king. Just as blond as Stewart, he had arms thick with muscle, his fingers long and fine. Twisted in his hands, not unlike the reins from the gallery painting she'd studied only hours before, were the dark lines of paint that led to an ancient queen. Around the pair of figures were dozens of the king's men of all shades and sizes. Their silver armor glinted in the sun, sword tips pointed at the queen, tangling with her long, dark hair.

Nim's eyes traced each line of the painting, again and again. The scene had been created in the style of a great conquest reproduced for the greatest dramatic effect, not historical accuracy, despite the details of the king's colors, crown, and rings. The robes were the very style the king of Inara would still wear. But the work was fanciful elsewhere, in strokes of motion among stillness, towers among a background of trees, and streaks of pink among a golden sky.

Attention returning to the dark lines knotted through the king's fingers, Nim reached out, her fingertip grazing the brushwork. The fine texture of layered paint thrummed beneath her touch, and she was closer, palms pressed flat, before her heart could even match its beat.

This, the magic said, *Here*. Her palm curled, nails clawing into the paint, cracking and raking free bits of pigment that made up tangled hair and lines of black. Beneath the tethers in the old king's hand, below that painted scene, waited another layer laced with an ancient power.

She stepped back, brushing the crackled pieces free, and stared at the tendrils of smoke that snaked over the panel and around the old queen's neck.

Magic. Darkness. The head of the Trust had been tethered by magic, bound to the catacombs of the undercity, and tied to the river of power that flowed beneath Inara, beneath the very castle that had been Nim's home.

CHAPTER 19

Margery stared at Rhen—self-proclaimed king of Inara, not some cursed magistrate—where he sat at Nim's desk, signing the orders Nim had agreed to put in place. He'd not outwardly done any harm with the dictates so far, but she wouldn't trust him farther than she could throw him. Though, to be fair, she would like to throw him very, very far.

"Lady Margery," he said without looking up from his task, "is there some assistance I can offer you?"

Her eyes narrowed, but she managed to bite down any retort.

Rhen dipped his quill into ink. "Very well, I do not mind if you merely lurk in the doorway." He gave her a fleeting sidelong glance. "You are well within your rights to ogle the king."

"I will not be goaded."

His lips twitched. "I wouldn't dare." He signed two more documents, sliding each to an edge of the desk, where the ink might dry, then glanced at her again. "The comment was meant with all sincerity. Ogle away."

"You are not a king."

He hummed, his lips tightening into something of a smile, like he was hiding a secret. She hated it.

She came into the room, stopping herself before quite reaching the desk. She crossed her arms to keep herself from shoving his work onto the floor in a fit of temper. "Why did Calum bargain to keep Warrick from the Trust?"

Rhen settled the quill in its place and looked up at her.

She lifted a shoulder, keeping her arms crossed. "You're bound from telling Nim but maybe not me."

"Why not you, do you suppose?"

"Maybe you owe me for your deceit. Maybe you weren't bound from speaking to someone with no association to the king." She leaned forward, just enough to plant a finger on a parchment resting on the desk. "Maybe you can write it down. I don't know. Find a way around it."

"I'm not certain I owe you—"

Her finger became a flattened palm as she leaned toward him threateningly.

He made a sound somewhere between a laugh and a throat clearing. "Lady Margery, what I said before is all that I am able—"

"Say it again. Now. For me."

He watched her for a moment, his gaze locked with hers, then his head inclined in a way that could only be taken as *anything for you*. She glared at him.

He leaned back in the chair as if considering how to word his reply. "Why wouldn't Calum want to keep Warrick out of the Trust?"

"Because Calum's place is secure. He's heir to the Trust, and everyone knows it. Warrick wasn't even raised by—" She stopped herself before she uttered *your kind* but only barely. Margery might want to tear the smirk off his face, but she'd never been tactless enough to call out a man for what couldn't be helped.

"Maybe there is more to it than all that."

She nodded. "I've heard whisperings. Discord among the higher-ups, a certain lack of support for the true heir."

Rhen was as still as stone.

"Is that what he fears, then? That your mother will hand Warrick the reins?"

"You are treading very near treachery, Lady Margery. I fear that words such as those might someday bring you peril."

"Not from you," she said.

His eyes glinted at the confidence in her tone. "Nonetheless. It is not a fate I would wish upon you."

She lifted her palm from the desk, straightening but not moving away. "Yet you act as if the fate you've all set upon us will end any better. And what of you? Hidden away entirely until that very heir was taken captive, bound by law and by bargain in the cells beneath our feet."

Rhen wet his lips. It was clear he wanted to respond. He could not—the bonds his mother had placed on him made it impossible. Everything about the situation was infuriating. She had a sudden overwhelming desire to smack the look he was giving her right off his face.

He let out a huff that might have been a laugh. "It won't help."

She stiffened. "What?"

"Being angry with me will not help."

She wondered if her desire had been so plain and made herself unclench her fist. "And yet it angers me all the same. Tell me something of use. You spent your whole life secreted away, and now you're here, you've crowned yourself king, and still you play games with Nim."

"You think very lowly of me, Lady Margery."

"Would that I could think of you not at all."

He bit his lip. "Perhaps—"

"Tell me something of use."

He crossed his hands over his chest, interlacing his fingers. "I've revealed all that I can, truly."

"Why, then, if Calum worked so very hard to keep Warrick from the Trust, has he bound him there now?" She leaned forward again. "What's different this time? What happens at Moontide?"

Any playfulness edging his expression and tone melted away. Rhen did not move, did not close the distance, but Margery felt the word as if he'd spoken it against her skin. "*Everything.*"

Margery had an unsettling desire to lean toward him more, to say what she truly thought, or to do something rash, something that could not be taken back.

"There's something you should know about me, Lady Margery." His voice was low, and she felt it suddenly deeper than her skin, as if its rumble were inside her chest.

"I have it." Nim's voice, bright, unexpected, and suddenly very near, snapped the tension between them, startling Margery to straighten to standing, her hand brushing the material of her gown into order though it had never been mussed at all.

For his part, Rhen looked momentarily as if he'd been caught at something, then his expression smoothed before he shook his head in confusion. "What?"

Nim's gaze darted between the two of them, but she was evidently too ruffled to pay any mind to whatever she'd walked into. "I am not precisely certain. But *something*."

Realization seemed to dawn on Rhen. He slid a hand over his vest, as if checking his pocket, then his attention went back to Nim. "Perhaps whatever you have is not something you would want to share with... everyone present."

Margery gaped at him, unsure whether she might throw the ink pot at his head or hit him with her bare flesh. "How dare you, you conniving no-good—"

Nim stepped forward. "Not you, Margery. He means him."

She looked back at Nim. "Oh. Of course. Honestly, Nimona, one wonders why you were sharing anything with him in the first place."

Nim ignored the remark, coming closer to the pair. "Warrick gave me a hint before. A clue he surely wanted me to find. And I keep thinking—I keep—"

"Nimona," Rhen warned.

The sound of her name in Rhen's level voice drew both women up short. They watched him silently. It was apparently the only advice he meant to give.

Nim nodded as if reading some unspoken message from Rhen's expression. "I won't reveal my plans. Only... I haven't figured those plans out yet. And Moontide is in days."

"One day."

Margery's stomach dropped at Rhen's response, the word he'd spoken earlier echoing in her head. *What happens at Moontide?* she'd asked. *Everything.*

Nim glanced at the darkened sky beyond the window, apparently unaware so much time had passed.

"You should rest, Majesty," Rhen said. "Perhaps it will come to you."

"You took us to the cells," Nim said, "and revealed the well of power runs even here."

Rhen shifted. "There is only so much I'm able to do, you understand."

"It hurts you," Nim said. "When I get too close to the answer. I can feel that you want to leave, that you need to distance yourself from it."

Margery didn't like what seemed to pass between them, and she had no intention of letting it slide. "What's going on?"

Nim's eyes didn't stray from Rhen. "I can feel it. Ever since I was bound to Warrick. I can feel what people want. It's the magic, its desire for sacrifice. Somehow, it allows me to sense the desires of others. So that whatever the desire is, it can be taken from them." After a moment, she added, "I can feel it in the same way they can: Warrick, Calum, and Rhen."

It was hard to say precisely how long the implications of the talent took to sink in, but when it did, Margery felt her face go hot. She could not help the glance she shot at Rhen.

His attention was already on her; he held her gaze. The flush slid further over her body. However aware he was of her,

Margery was surely a thousand times more aware of him. As such, something became suddenly clear to her. Something she'd seen in the king's sepulcher. A tell she should have become aware of far earlier in their acquaintance. They had no time to dally about.

To Nim, she said only, "No more secrets, remember."

Her voice was steadier than she might have hoped for, but her hands trembled when she crossed around the narrow desk to stand before Rhen. The barest scent of him—sandalwood and woodruff—rose from his vest as she took hold of him, gripping hard as she brought him painfully near her face. She was by no means short, but she'd not had to lean as far as she ought to bring them eye to eye.

"Lady Margery..." He sounded bemused, maybe a little wary.

Margery tried very hard to keep the desire she'd focused on at the top of her list. It was not a great deal of trouble, it turned out, because his slow exhalation brushed over her face, touching her lips, teasing her closer to him still. She lingered just long enough that he softened, that his mouth went lax for what must have been want of words.

Then she snatched her hands back, spun over the desk, and landed beside Nim, as quick as a snake.

CHAPTER 20

Margery alighted beside Nim with a grace that nearly put Maris to shame. Nim thought for maybe a moment she might have misread her friend, the way she'd lingered so long in the region of Rhen's person, but both she and Rhen understood before Margery's feet had hit the ground that he'd been well and truly played. Nim could not make out the way Rhen felt about it, only that he meant to act.

Paper crumpled in Margery's hand as Nim drew her sword. In two heartbeats, Rhen was standing. Nim pointed her weapon at his neck, Margery tucked behind her with the folded note she'd pulled from his vest.

He'd kept touching it, Nim realized, brushing his hands over it as if checking it was there, like some nervous tic. Fates, but she was a fool. She'd missed it time and again.

"Lady Margery, this is no game." Rhen's voice was frigid, the warning in it patent. "If you do not return that document to my possession, I will have no choice but to come for it. With force if necessary."

Margery told him to sod off.

The tip of Nim's sword touched his throat.

"Even you, Nim. I have no choice."

"Regrettable," Nim said.

Rhen closed his eyes then took a measured breath. When he moved, his speed put Margery's to shame. He had leapt over the desk, disarmed Nim, and laid Margery flat on her back beneath him before the tick of a clock.

"Get *off* me."

Margery's face was flushed, but Nim didn't think she'd been hurt. Rhen clearly had the parchment back in his hand, but he stayed above her, giving her a long look.

"Your treachery could cost you greatly, Lady Margery. I ask you to remember that."

Nim, meanwhile, had scrambled to her feet and managed to get her hands on the sword. She raised it over Rhen's head.

He didn't even glance up at her as his magic knocked her onto her rear.

"She's a queen, you—" Margery struggled beneath Rhen, muttering dark insults about everything from his character to his person.

"Indecorous of you, Lady Margery," Rhen replied. "Perhaps you should save such talk for when we are not in the presence of others."

Nim had managed to release the dagger at her thigh, but she no more than had a solid grip before Rhen was standing, giving her a disappointed glance, and tugging Margery to her feet.

"Ladies, I believe I've had enough for one evening." He released Margery's hand, shoved the crumpled parchment back into his vest pocket, then managed a mostly elegant bow. "Good night."

Margery stared after him for a long while. Nim, exhausted, put off that she'd been so easily disarmed and thoroughly vexed that she was stuck with Rhen when she needed no one so much as Warrick, sorted her wardrobe and desk back into order.

When Margery finally moved, she placed a hand over Nim's, stalling her erratic shuffling of the papers. "I will handle this.

Please. Go and clean up, say good night to Allister. We've a big day tomorrow, and you need to get your head clear."

Nim met her gaze. The understanding there nearly caused her heart to break. Margery was right. Nim needed to think about what she'd learned. She needed sleep.

She sighed. "I don't deserve you."

Margery patted her hand. "As you've said. Now go."

Nim righted a ceramic dish as her final act of creating order, and Margery settled into the chair.

"In the morning," Nim said. "We will talk."

Margery smiled at her then went back to her work.

It wasn't until dawn came in through the windows to her suite that Nimona realized Margery had never agreed.

CHAPTER 21

Margery was gone. She'd stayed up late, quill scratching on parchment as Nim dozed off on a settee in the sitting room. Not wanting to face their room when he was gone, Nim had not returned to Warrick's suite. It was foolish, likely, given that it was where Warrick had wanted her to be. But she'd chosen to stay near Allister and Alice, with Margery.

She cursed.

"Majesty." Alice's voice was low beside her, more agreement than censure. She glanced up at Nim. "What should we do?"

"We can't go searching for her," Wes said. They both looked at him, and he hurried to explain. "She left of her own free will, sneaked out on purpose, and... well, it's Moontide Day."

Nim cursed again. It was Moontide. The day of the trial. Her one chance to help Warrick, and she didn't have a hope in the world. All she had was a string of clues that, in the light of day, felt so much less like a true discovery and so much more like a tangled web. And Rhen with his cursed hints. Her mind could not help but search those clues again. The first time she'd encountered Rhen, she had the sense he'd been teasing some secret just out of her reach. But Nim had had no chance to find out what it was before she stabbed him.

When she'd escaped, Warrick had seemed furious—and looking back, it might have been more. It might have been that she'd been forced to use a dagger that would cost him gains he'd made against the Trust.

The rest she didn't know. She couldn't understand why Rhen had dragged her to her father's cell or what she was missing. He'd approached her at the ball and warned her not to react, lest she be caught by the king. She'd accused him of coming for Calum, and he had answered smoothly, *You think I desire the return of my eldest brother? That I would await his homecoming only to watch him take his place before me as heir?* He was too clever for that, he'd said. Then he had offered, *Let me keep you. A trophy to hold over both my brothers. And in return, you will be left alive.*

That is the bargain I offer. It is you, or it is Warrick.

He'd been toying with Warrick and with her. But he'd drawn her into the Trust regardless of everything else. He'd drawn her there, and she'd stood before his mother and, when Nim had begged her not to hurt Warrick, had sworn to give herself instead, the head of the Trust had said *I already have you.*

For his mother. Rhen had done it for her. Because she'd left him with no other choice.

Maris eyed the wall near the hidden panel, apparently still searching for clues of Margery's disappearance. But Margery knew her way around well enough to avoid being caught if she didn't mean to.

"Rhen's gone too," Bramwell said. "Garrett followed him to the square, where he met with a handful of Trust accountants before dawn. Couldn't discover what they might have been up to, but no doubt they were friendly to his cause."

Nim sighed, sliding down into the chair with an urge to drop her head to the desk. She'd slept fitfully, a night full of dreams, and had woken with a good deal more dread for what was coming. "I don't know what to do. I can't—"

Her words cut off as she caught sight of Margery's handwriting, a hasty scrawl that Margery would never use for a document she meant anyone to see. It wasn't an official document at all. It was a note for Nim.

"What is it?"

She'd not realized her breath had drawn so hard until the concern in Wes's tone snapped her back. She glanced up at him then back at the parchment, sliding the layer from the top to see more notes. She cursed a third time, and before she'd even had her tea.

"The paper," she said. "The fate-forsaken paper she stole out of Rhen's vest."

Wes, Maris, Alice, and Bramwell stood staring at her.

Nim let loose a wild laugh, too loud and bright. Margery must have read the paper in the scant moments before Rhen had seized it back from her. The words were scratched out and scribbled; her frantic scrawling in the middle of the night must have been her attempt to recall what she'd seen, to piece it together. For Nim.

Margery had done it. She'd finally given them something of use.

"It's a contract," Nim explained, hands shaking where she held the pages covered in Margery's notes. "Stewart's contract with the queen." She stood slowly, feeling unstable and entirely discomposed. The terms. She had King Stewart's contract terms.

"Fate save us," Nim managed. "We have the queen."

CHAPTER 22

They did not have the head of the Trust, not yet. Margery moved as quickly as she was able through the back alleys and less-used streets of Inara, gathering what she needed to do a foolish thing. She had understood Rhen's words deeply, felt their truth in just the way he'd meant her to.

What she was doing was more than treacherous. It could not be helped.

The rising sun had crossed over the kingdom as she worked, its shadows growing shorter toward midday with the counting of time. Moontide had arrived, Warrick would face a trial come sunset, and Inara stood to lose not only its last true king but its freedom as well.

Margery meant to have none of it.

CHAPTER 23

The carriage came to a stop before the gates to the undercity. The rattle of hoof, harness, and wheel echoed with an unsettling sense of finality—though that feeling may have only been the awareness of Rhen's emotions where he sat across from Nim. The inside of the carriage felt too confined, though Rhen seemed to have tied both his intimations and himself together tidily enough. He wore the robes of an Inaran king, along with Stewart's overlarge signet ring on the hand that rested over his knee. He said nothing, his eyes on her.

Nim squeezed Wes's hand where his fingers wound through hers. She'd wanted to leave him, to make him stay inside the castle with Alice and Allister, where he might be safe from a dark queen's clutches, but she could not. He was owed being present, the same as she, and in truth, no place would be safe for him should the worst come to pass. At her side, opposite Wes, was the sword that had been bought with his father's bargain.

Outside, Maris and Bramwell leapt down from the carriage then opened its door to the red glow of a dying day. The sun would dip completely below the buildings soon then disappear with what was left of their freedom. Fates, it was hard to be

139

anything but morose. At least the dread was keeping the rest at bay.

"Majesty." Maris's tone was solemn as she slipped her sword back into its sheath.

The king's guard on horseback slid to the ground, forming up as their current king and queen alighted from the carriage.

Rhen stopped beside Nim, offering an arm. She gave him a quelling look, and the tension broke from him. A genuine smile came and went across his expression like a stray wind. "Your Majesty," he told her solemnly, "it has been an intense pleasure to know you, from the start."

Given that she'd stabbed him fairly early in their acquaintance, the sentiment seemed unlikely. Then again, she supposed compared to Calum, such a straightforward attack might feel like a gift.

Nim drew back her shoulders, preparing to stride to her doom. "May our acquaintance last beyond this sunset."

He made a sound in his throat, keeping pace beside her as if she were not about to walk from Inara and the sunset sky for the last time.

The king's guard watched, a few dozen remaining posted by the carriage, a few more falling in line behind the group. Before them, the gates were raised and torches lit with unnatural flame in anticipation of the coming dark. Trust men and women stood at attention in full uniform, eyes alight with a similar unsettling glow. Their intimations bit at Nim, anticipation sharp, senses ablaze with the power that swam from beneath the stones at their feet. It called to her, strangely, in neither the lulling sensations nor the stinging fear, sparking through the air around her, but not smothering. Not yet.

It needs you closer.

Nim's attention snapped to Rhen, unsure whether the thought had been his or hers, but his gaze was forward, his bearing steady as he strode through the archway and into the main corridor.

A handful of well-dressed Trust associates escorted them through the undercity's halls and corridors, deep into the bowels, where the magic was most dense. It was a heavy weight around them, still hovering, as if in wait. Rhen was quiet, not addressing a single Trust associate along the route. They watched, some dipping into a bow, some inclining their heads, some making no move at all.

At a pair of double doors, he seemed to shift, standing taller, hands posed carefully about his waist, though she had no idea what he might mean to seize with them. A dagger would do little good against what waited beyond in the chamber. It didn't stop her own hand from itching for the grip of the sword at her side, though.

"Majesty," purred a tall woman with dark curls and a golden glint to her eyes as she opened the door for Rhen.

Nim could not tell whether the look was mocking or friendly, only that Rhen's next step brought him closer to Nim.

They entered a chamber that rose impossibly high, its rafters crisscrossing through open space that seemed lit from above. The space was so large that it took Nim's breath. Her step faltered as the true immensity of the queen's realm came into view. In her tasks for Calum, Nim had only seen the rooms he'd wanted her to see. He'd only given her access to their secrets when it had benefited him. Clearly, he'd kept her far from anything beyond the court-like atmosphere of his mother's rule. Or, perhaps, he'd only meant to keep his games with Nim from Trust view.

Rhen's arm brushed hers, as if casually, and Nim resumed her composure with a swallowed curse. It seemed impossible that she was beneath Inara, unfathomable that she'd never known such splendor existed below the kingdom.

"You've been keeping secrets," she murmured to Rhen.

"Curious that it would surprise you at this point," he said.

She felt Wes and Maris behind her but could not guess whether they gaped openly. She imagined Maris might be wearing more of a scowl. She yearned for Margery, to share with her—but no, she could not yearn for that. Because if she had one more chance to see Margery, it would be only to say goodbye. Nim felt well and truly done for.

Murmuring picked up as they came through the gathered crowd. Figures moved from shadowed corners into the misty light in the center of what she realized was a massive throne room. Nim's stomach sank as they kept on. Endless steps led through endless faces, endless intimations, past open pits on the floor that swam with the source of the magic, too strong, too near, too endless in its power. Before them, across the ceaseless space, was a dais that was familiar only in that she'd seen one before. The thrones of Inaran kings had never been so great as the monstrosity that held the head of the Trust.

The word was unfair even as she thought it, because the throne itself was a marvel. The piece of stonework had surely been created by the greatest craftsmen who'd ever lived, over lifetimes of toiling on nothing but it, because such was precisely how the Trust operated. Men would bargain for the skill to build remarkable things, then their bargains would cost them in ways that prevented their boon from becoming useful in any manner. Except if it was useful to the Trust, of course.

What made it monstrous was not its grandeur but what it held. Upon the dark and imposing throne sat Warrick's mother, head of the Trust and possessor of the fate for all whom Nim held dear.

Nim's thoughts stumbled, but she had no chance to decide whether the thought of holding one's fate had come from herself or Rhen.

"Nimona Weston," the head of the Trust said.

All in attendance fell silent, a strange stillness sweeping the room.

"I am queen," Nim said, because truly, she had nothing else to weight her place.

The head of the Trust chuckled. Beside her, Calum sat tall in a seat of his own, his posture not the easy grace Nim had come to know. At each side stood a half dozen Trust associates, their dress seeming to indicate positions of importance—and hideous wealth.

"Where is Warrick?" She could not call him king, not while Rhen wore Stewart's signet ring and the title with it.

The head of the Trust's mouth shifted into something that spoke of pleasure, but Nim sensed nothing of the sort from her. "The prisoner will be brought forth when his own trial begins."

Rhen's hand slid over Nim's back before she realized she'd taken a step backward. Wes came to her other side, his hand gripping into the fabric over her ribs, keeping her safe from magic.

"What are you playing at, Mother?" Rhen asked levelly.

The head of the Trust paid him no mind, her eyes on Nim alone. "First, we must deal with those who conspired with him, breakers of bargains and conspirators against the Trust." The edge of her mouth curled upward, and the sense of Calum's pleasure swam over Nim. "Guards," the head of the Trust said, "bring them forward."

CHAPTER 24

Wes's grip was all that kept Nim upright when a group of prisoners was marched to stand before the dais. The head of the Trust gestured, and despite Rhen's protests, Trust guards herded Nim, Wes, and Maris closer. A sound came out of Wes that might have broken Nim's heart had she not been sick already. Cloth sacks covered the figures' heads, but their wardrobes made clear they were agents of Inara. King's colors trimmed one's guard uniform. The robes of a clerk draped over another. There was no question what had drawn the sound of distress from Wesley.

The fourth in line was wearing a familiar dress—one they'd all seen only the night before. It was Margery, her fine gown torn at sleeve and skirt, something dark smearing her bound hands.

The sickness nearly overwhelmed Nim, twisting shock into betrayal then utter fury. It boiled within her, too hot and strong, before Nim realized it was not wholly hers. She glanced back at Rhen. He'd been separated from her, his dark eyes upon his mother. Color had risen up his neck, rage hardening his always-playful features into something almost unrecognizable.

"Everyone," the head of the Trust said distinctly, "pays when conspiring against the Trust and its head."

Rhen's answering intimation seemed to be a vow, though Nim's attention was drawn from it as the hoods were jerked from the heads of those in line.

Nim imagined herself hitting the ground, her knees cracking against the stone floor, Wes tugged down to kneel beside her as she wept. But she stood, defeated and distraught, holding on to the last shred of control, barely managing not to give in. Among the prisoners was a trembling Lady Lora, lords and ladies Nim only recognized in passing, and Margery's cousin Beasley, who'd been stripped down to shirt and trousers.

Margery's head was held high, her gaze unapologetic.

What have you done? Nim wanted to ask. Nim could not. Nim was queen.

"Enough with this foolishness." The feverish edge to her voice couldn't be helped. "What grounds could you possibly have to charge any of them?"

Beasley was practically a layabout. Half the time, he couldn't be bothered to attend gatherings that were held in his own family manor. They'd only taken him because of Nim's friendship with Margery, surely. The charges could not be legitimate.

The head of the Trust smiled. "They were caught here, in fact, bargaining away to save their newly crowned queen in our own domain."

Nim went cold. "Margery."

The word slipped out as no more than a whisper, but in the silence of the room, the despair in it felt like a scream.

Margery wet her lips but did not speak.

Rhen closed the distance the Trust guards had made between him and Nim, coming to stand beside her. "Your games grow old. The day grows late. Get on with it, Mother."

Nim felt the head of the Trust's irritation at Rhen's words, but she could not pick out precisely why. Too many intimations rushed over her, the power beneath her feet a current of its own, and her heart a shattered mess. Inara was done for. The Trust would have the kingdom and with it everything Nim held dear, all of it taken apart before her eyes. She suspected the utter conviction of her failure was coming from the queen, but the knowledge it might not be her own didn't lessen Nim's grief.

"Look at them," Rhen said. "Lowly citizens on parade as if you did not have the kingdom's highest already bound."

"Lowly indeed." The head of the Trust smiled. "And yet mine all the same. With their bargains, I own these paltry citizens, even as they attempt to use those bargains against the Trust." She paused, her gaze lingering on Rhen. "Interesting, is it not? That I now own the Lady Ayer, the same as I owned her father."

Margery held impossibly still as Rhen replied conversationally, "Is that so? And what has she bargained for that could possibly bring harm to the Trust?"

The head of the Trust flicked a hand, voice sharp. "Take her first. The gallows, I think, just the way it's done in Inara."

Nim lurched forward, hand outstretched. "No" tore from her involuntarily. Wes held firmer, keeping her from an attempt that would see Nim hanged as well.

"No?" the head of the Trust said incredulously. "What would you prefer, *lady queen*? Something slower, more painful? Perhaps you'll wish me to give her to my eldest instead."

Beside her, Calum stared on, uncharacteristically quiet. But in his eyes, the desire for a slow and cruel reckoning was plain.

Nim swallowed. "She's to face a trial, is she not? What farce have you brought us to witness if she's only to submit to judgment on a whim? I demand just proceedings or none at all."

"Ha!" She shifted in her seat, throne or no, irritation spiking through intimations she was plainly trying to keep under control. "You *demand?*"

Nim stepped forward, one pace closer to Margery and to the queen. "I demand." She glanced at the watching crowd. "As queen of Inara, I hold you to your own bargain, to the ties set between the Trust and the kingdom long ago."

Nim had no idea if her threat would hold any weight, but the rage that boiled up in the head of the Trust had her wanting to scramble backward. She found an embarrassing attempt at escape was not a concern, after all, because she was frozen in place. Power wrapped around her, threatening to press the air from her lungs and burn every surface of her skin. The accompanying intimation showed her exactly how it would feel should the boy behind her, protecting her from the magic, be removed from her touch. Nim bit down against a scream, unsure if anyone else in the room could know what the queen was doing.

"Enough." Rhen's voice was a command. "She is right, is she not? Rules are in place. The Trust is *nothing* without those rules."

His words held some deeper meaning, but Nim could not make it out, gasping for breath as she was. Wes inched closer, murmuring his concern, Nim thought, but when she looked back at him, she realized his eyes were on Margery. Fates save them all, she couldn't decipher what they meant to do.

"Please," she started, but another command from the queen snapped her attention back.

"Yes. The Trust is nothing without its rules." She stood and sauntered down the steps of the dais. "Bring the true prize of tonight's game."

Prize, her son, the very man she'd placed upon the throne of Inara, only to tear down later and usurp with another heir. Bitter words rose to Nim's lips, but she managed not a single one when the doors beyond the dais swung open, the sound echoing through the cavernous space.

CHAPTER 25

Warrick walked through the massive doorway under his own power, emerging from a shadowed corridor that Nim could only hope didn't lead to a cell. His hands were bound before him, a bruise marred the side of his brow, and his fine clothes had been replaced with a plain black shirt and trousers. A line of guards flanked him. His gaze was for Nim alone.

Wes held firm to the material at the back of Nim's bodice, preventing her from involuntarily moving forward. Warrick was still bound by magic and unable to send intimations, but his gaze promised he would not be bound for long.

"Stop there." The warning in the queen's voice threw icy water on the relief Nim had allowed herself at seeing Warrick.

He came to a standstill upon the dais. Four guards were all that separated him from Calum. Four guards and the untold power that secured his magical bindings.

The head of the Trust shifted. "To remind you of the stakes, *Majesty.*"

There was no ambiguity in her tone. She meant to punish Nim, and she did not for a moment recognize her as a true queen of Inara.

That was fine, Nim supposed, because Nim had put no stock in Rhen being Inara's king either. "I am well aware of the stakes. Though I have little faith in these trials being just."

The glint in the head of the Trust's eyes said fairness was the least of her concern. "This is how it will go," she answered. "The evidence against Warrick will be presented for all to see, without question, that he is guilty of his crime. Conspiracy against the Trust and its head is a grave offense, punishable by death." Her gown slid over her as she moved, light catching on the material in a manner reminiscent of the body of the snake they'd sent to strike Nim. Her slender hands were graceful even in stillness, her bare arms a proclamation of lean strength. Everything about the woman screamed *threat*, even as she vowed to do her worst. "And so you will be left with a choice. As queen of Inara, you may give your life for his."

Warrick's life or Nim's. She had been given the choice before. She had chosen him. A thousand times, she would choose him. The head of the Trust knew it. It was why she'd created this game.

Her gaze met Nim's, making clear the queen was well pleased. The bargain Nim's father had made so very long ago was playing out, to no one's surprise, in the wrong queen's favor.

Nim was to decide the fate of the heir. To save Warrick, she would have to sacrifice herself. Then Warrick would take vengeance on the queen. Inara would be thrown to the wolves. That was what the bargains did—gave the bettor precisely what they'd asked in the antithesis of their true desires. Her father had meant to save Inara and its king by giving Nim the power to decide. But she was Inara's queen, and standing before her on the dais, his wrists in chains, was its true king. One of them would die. The other would fight. Inara would fall. The sacrifices and bargains made by so many had never held a chance to save the kingdom at all.

Wes slipped his hand into hers. For a moment, she was barely aware of the contact. Then he pressed his fingers tightly around hers, and she felt something hard against her palm. He had no intimations, but she understood as plainly as if Wes had spoken. *This*, the gesture said, *is important. This, they cannot see.* She drew a slow breath, feeling the object with the pad of her thumb when his hand withdrew from hers.

The token was small and round, its edges nicked, its surface embossed with soft lines. She understood because she'd held it before, cherished it as the last possession of a man she'd loved. Her heart kicked, pulse growing to a rhythm that the magic couldn't match. Rhen had tried to show her, tried to show them all.

Nim's voice rang loud over the silence of the watching crowd. "Where is the boon Lady Margery received in the trade she's been accused of?"

Calum's gaze snapped to Nim's, but the head of the Trust only looked on as if she'd not heard the demand.

"The boon," Nim repeated.

The queen did not look at her. "Lady Ayer is a prisoner of the Trust. She belongs to *me*."

"She belongs to no one."

"She stands accused. Her crime was witnessed. She is hereby found guilty. She belongs to the Trust evermore or until her death."

"If you charge her for conspiring based on the bargain made, then her contract must have been sealed. She made the deal." Nim stepped forward, Wes close at her back. "She has no heir but the kingdom of Inara. And I, as queen, claim the debt as my own."

"You could never pay it," Calum hissed. He'd come to his feet as if unintentionally.

Nim's gaze flicked to Margery in time to see her mouth curl into something wicked. "Him?" Nim whispered, stare shifting to Calum. "You made your bargain with *him*?"

Calum's expression went impossibly harder. "This is none of your concern."

It was very much her concern, she realized. Whatever was happening beyond her understanding, she could sense she'd found a weakness in Calum's conviction. He'd been so certain he was about to see Nim meet her reckoning, that he would finally win.

"I demand the boon, by the laws of the Trust. Lady Margery's debt is mine."

Calum seemed about to launch himself forward from the dais. Rhen snapped a gesture at the guard, but they only moved closer to Warrick, who seemed to be fighting his invisible restraints.

"You cannot refuse her in this," Rhen warned. "And if you try, then I, *as king of Inara*, can make the demand on her behalf." His intimation was a challenge to the others in the room, but it crept over Nim's skin like the air before a lightning strike. "If none of you recall our laws, then leave it to me to remind you."

Trust procedures were not complicated when it came to the transfer of debt. There would be no way to deny Nim the request, even if she had not been queen. Margery had no heir. But Nim *was* queen, and with Rhen at her side and the Trust watching, Calum had no choice.

He knew it. But there was a moment of uncertainty, a heartbeat in which Nim thought Calum might delay delivery of the trade, that the head of the Trust might decide to move forward with Margery's punishment before she handed over Margery's boon. Instead, one of Calum's men came down from the dais, walked behind Margery, and cut loose her binds.

Nim's heart hammered. Margery seemed impervious. She reached into her bodice without so much as taking a moment to stretch her unbound hands, yanked a crumpled roll of parchment from beneath—where it had apparently been smashed against her ribs—then tossed it across the space to Nim.

Before she could make another move, the head of the Trust

said, "There," as if, deed done, Margery's neck might be cut, as quickly as that. And, indeed, it was that quick. A blade rose behind her, a Trust guard's hand slipping up to steady her shoulder, his other poised to strike before Nim had managed to form a word.

"Hold." Rhen's voice cracked through the space like the lightning his intimation had promised only moments before, the magic laced within stopping the guard cold.

The head of the Trust's laugh was as sharp as a blade. "And there, all of it revealed for the world to see." She strode closer in a slow, snaking path, her pleasure and hatred patent, even without the benefit of the cruel intimations. But send the intimations she did, again and again, to both Nim and Rhen. "My heir," she purred. "Third son and child of an Inaran king." She *tsked* at him as if he were a naughty child. "We all see now where your loyalties lie." She turned to the watching crowd, voice growing louder for all to hear. "It seems Stewart has given my boys a perverse interest in the ladies of Inara. Shame that I own them both."

The dread in Nim's gut at how close Margery had come to meeting a bloody end had nearly distracted her from reason. But she had no time for fear. Hands trembling, she fumbled the scroll while the head of the Trust moved closer.

The queen's approach did not stop near Rhen, an intimation from her making clear she would deal with him soon. Instead, she came closer still, her gaze raking over Nim and the contract, her dark eyes laughing when they landed on the seal. "The contract is yours, truly, along with its debt, and yet without Trust blood, that seal can never be broken."

Rhen shifted, his grab like the strike of a snake, but as fast as it was, he never laid hands on the contract. The queen's magic cracked through the air, less like lightning and more like the swift snap of a solid bone. Desire rose in Nim, even as her feet shuffled backward. Wes closed in behind her, wrapping tighter to her, and they both stared on at Rhen, who had been thrown to the floor.

He writhed for only a moment then coughed. He slid a hand to his chest, which rose and fell jerkily as he fought to breathe. Several of the prisoners struggled against their bonds. Warrick cursed. Calum's emotions swelled past his usual shield, letting everyone present know exactly how he felt about his brother's suffering.

Rhen spoke something soft for only his mother to hear. His blood pooled then made a slow path across the floor toward Nim's feet. That blood, Nim realized, could be used to break a magical seal. She lunged.

With Wes clinging to her for all he was worth, the queen's magic could not touch Nim. But the queen was clever and no mere human in strength or speed. She slammed into Nim, aware of her plan and putting an end to it before it had fully taken root.

Her hand was a vise around the meat of Nim's arm, dragging her backward. "His blood will never help you." She was too close, her voice a hiss of breath against Nim's skin as her fingers clawed through the material of Nim's sleeve. "For even you, foolish girl, understand that a contract's bond cannot be fully broken while its token remains in Trust hands."

Nim let her press closer, allowing the threat in the queen's words to simmer with the magic that bit through Nim's palms. *Too close.* Nim's flesh felt alive with the magic; it was crawling about her like a second skin. Her eyes fell closed as she sank into it, lulled by the whispered promises even as the magic swore to devour.

Nim. Warrick's voice thrummed through her, accompanied by the sensation of his fingers crossing slowly over the exposed flesh of her neck. The queen's grip tightened into Nim's arm, drawing blood.

Nim's eyes snapped open. Warrick stared back at her from the dais, a half dozen Trust guards holding him in place. It was not fear she read in his gaze.

The queen jerked Nim's arm to break the connection. Up

close, she was perfect. Her skin was flawless, her lips smooth and rich in color. But her eyes were depthless, something dark and irredeemable inside.

Nim's voice was low, the calm threat in it almost unrecognizable to her own ears. "My father wanted nothing more than for me—for all of us—to be free from you. From the Trust and its magic. For years, I thought that his bargain, like so many others, had cost him the very thing he had wished to win. The same as Wes and his sword, the same as Stewart and his heirs. I thought that the magic called to me in some cruel twist of fate, that corrupt binds had been put on us to keep the boon from my father's reach."

It didn't matter that Nim had never bargained herself—she'd been tied by contract nonetheless. Her freedom had been theirs for nearly as long as she could remember. She had not been the only one. "He wanted me to destroy the magic, the Trust. And all I could do was let it draw me in. I know now what each of their sacrifices meant for me. I understand, as you say, exactly how a token works."

She held up the hand that wore a thin silver band—a sacrifice from her mother, given to her as a wedding band by Warrick. The silver glinted in the shafts of moonlight that fell, impossibly, from somewhere above. Her other hand slipped smoothly over Wes's blade tucked against her side, a weapon not simply sharp but imbued with magic that had once belonged to the head of the Trust. It cut fast and deep, and she had to fist her hand to keep the blood from running free. She pressed the fist to her thigh, hoping to buy a moment before the head of the Trust realized what she'd done.

But it didn't matter. Not any longer.

"You think you'll win." Nim leaned forward, seething, voice a low hiss. "That every sacrifice made in the name of protecting Inara can be bought by the flick of your wrist." Her mouth curved cruelly; it couldn't be helped. She wanted to bludgeon the woman before her with a violence she'd never imagined possible. "But I know your secret, *lady queen*."

Nim moved forward another step, fingers curled so tightly into her palms, she might have drawn blood from that alone. "I know precisely why you need me." She let her face inch closer, her words a whisper for only the head of the Trust to hear. "I know how to break your terms."

CHAPTER 26

The reaction from the head of the Trust was immediate and brutal. Nim was unceremoniously torn from Wes's grip. Her body hit the floor lengths away, where she landed with a muffled crack. Distantly, she knew her skull had hit the stone far too heavily. Further still, she was aware of the watching crowd closing in and the figures on the dais coming to stand. The head of the Trust was breaking an ancient covenant.

Nim was breaking terms of her own. She did not have the blood of the Trust, but she understood now that she did not need it. Her father had given her something far more precious—a connection to the magic. Nim's bloodied hand closed around the contract, fracturing a seal that had been set when she was but a girl. The scent of her childhood memories rose through her with feelings of warmth and promise—of what she missed most when she'd forced herself not to think of them, when the magic had tried to use those desires against her.

Calum had not broken her father's contract when he'd given Nim the debt. Her father had made a bargain with the head of the Trust. Calum had written a new contract for Nim—one that had only listed his terms. One that had held a lock of Nim's girlhood hair inside.

From this contract fell a lock of her father's hair, lighter than Nim's and with a hint of curl. It tumbled to the stone beside her, stone that was damp with her blood. She drew a ragged breath, bathing in the love she felt sewn inside his terms. *Her*. They had done it all for *her*. Some part of Nim wanted to argue that no, they'd done it for Inara, but she could think of nothing at all once the magic broke free.

Across the space, the head of the Trust, in all her savage majesty, struck poor Wesley to the floor. She could not use magic against him, but it was clear she did not need to. She turned toward Nim as if sensing the contract had broken just as Nim's hand dropped limply to the floor. Her palm fell open, and the coin that had been her father's token rolled slowly across the stones.

The head of the Trust roared, the sound rumbling through the throne room and knocking dust to rain through the vast space between lofty ceiling and palatial floor. A voice spoke beneath the din, only for Nim. *You have broken the contract. His debt is paid*. And with it, she understood that her father had won his boon. Finally, free and clear. It was his.

Then she realized the voice had been Warrick's. He was free of his bonds. Even as she lay broken, his magic was putting her back together. Nim pushed unsteadily up to sit just as a dark and powerful queen threw herself across the space, intent on murder.

Warrick slammed into his mother, their bodies colliding along with their magic, and Nim was thrown back with the force of the impact. Calum rushed from the dais, Trust guards and accountants swarming closer along with him. Nim flinched as something brushed her arm. Soothing words followed, and she turned to find Wes, battered and disheveled, something bright in his gaze. *Hope*, she might have thought, if she could get her fool brain to catch up at all.

He shoved a familiar mace into her hands. It was Nim's, the one she'd carried for years, except that it felt somehow less familiar. The weapon hummed against her palm, just as the magic thrummed beneath her feet.

Her father's contract was broken. His boon was Nim's to command. "Help me," she whispered, and Wes dragged them both ungainly to their feet. "Save Margery."

Nim did not need his protection. Not any longer. He gave her arm a final squeeze then rushed away as Nim took a staggering step forward. Warrick and his mother were locked in battle, the magic's violence visceral as it wrapped about them. It would have dragged Nim closer had she not been moving toward it of her own will. Her hand tightened on the mace, her feet another step closer, her focus solely on Warrick and the head of the Trust.

Calum's blow caught her completely off guard. He'd not bothered with the cane or magic—though Wes's protection was nowhere near. He'd struck her with a bare fist. The impact reverberated through her bones, leaving her ear hot and ringing and her already-unsteady balance in worse shape yet. She reeled sideways, her focus coming back slowly to a fuzzy Rhen dragging himself from the floor several lengths away, Trust accountants fighting among themselves, and Calum's personal guard closing the distance. She blinked hard and stumbled. Calum moved again.

He grabbed hold of the thin cloak at her shoulder, yanking her to him with an ugly sneer. Gone were the usual airs, no hint of his station in his bearing. Pure fury radiated from him, his intimation burning through any lingering effects of the blow. Nim was in trouble—not that she hadn't been before—but Calum meant to kill her imminently.

"It's come to this." Her words were thick, and she had no idea what she was saying, only that she might buy herself time. Calum had loved nothing more than a good game, but the look he was giving her did not bode well for her plan to reach that side of him.

"It's come to the end." His sneer somehow managed to become uglier, and he tugged her closer, dragging her upward so that her feet barely touched the floor.

Nim sucked in a breath, thinking of nothing so much as her father's love. It was hard, not merely because she'd spent so many years avoiding it but because it hurt. Breaking the seal of the contract had ripped open the old wound. She felt her heart rend even as the desire for magic swelled within her, the ancient power calling to her in the way it always did. She seized hold of the connection.

A flickering of torchlight heralded the magic's waking, the lulling pulse she'd always known suddenly alive and biting as it sang through her limbs. Calum seemed to sense it, his face changing and his grip growing slack.

Nim's boots touched the stone as the sleepy mist stirred, twisting higher and twitching in time to the pulse of the magic, licking at the air, eager for its tithe. A breathless laugh rose from Nim unbidden. Power climbed over her, the writhing of snakes no more. It swelled and crested, lifting her hair and crackling against her weapons. Its tingling heat awaited command.

Calum called her a very nasty word. Then he lunged, cane raised, but Nim was faster. She dodged to the side, mace in hand, and thrust every scrap of power she could into its blow.

The muted crack could only have been the sound of breaking bone. She didn't wait, rearing back to strike again. Calum drove toward her, shoulder first, and slammed them both to the ground. They rolled, knocked into the steps of the dais, then grappled to their feet. She swung at him again, hitting square and true, and he stumbled backward over the steps. He was upright before a breath, his own magic rising like the tide.

Nim edged away, but he followed her forward, the magic he'd called at his back promising to end her as clearly as if it had spoken the words. It was too much. Nim could feel it.

"Calum." Her word was only a whisper, and she wasn't sure

whether it was a warning or something more. It did nothing to stop him.

He released his magic, throwing the wave of power at her with everything he had. He meant to end her once and for all.

Nim's hands came up on instinct, the power singing through her so much a part of her that she never paused to think. The magic rose to meet his, impossibly, crashing into itself with the warring desire of each of its conduits. Calum was stronger. He had magic in his blood. As heir to the Trust, he was more powerful than anyone aside from his mother.

His assault should have crushed her. It did not. She had only an instant to read his reaction, to see his expression shift and feel his intimation slip from lethal to stunned. Only an instant, because that was all it took before his magic crashed to the ground at his feet, sinking through the stones and into the well of power beneath them once more.

When the magic rose again, it was with pure vengeance. Calum had spent every bit of power he could gather, thrown it away on a single, useless blow. He had taken more than he could pay for. Magic always had a cost.

He stared at her, understanding slow to come. He had meant to take the queen of Inara, to collect her pain and her blood as a sacrifice to pay the toll. But Nim was not of the Trust. She did not have to play by their rules. The laws of magic had been bent to allow her access, the cost of that access paid by her father's sacrifice.

Nim owed nothing for the power she used.

The head of the Trust let out a cry of denial and despair, but it was too late for even her to help him. *Magic cannot be given freely*, they had always said. Nim had just discovered why. Before her eyes, the vigor was taken out of Calum. Like Nim's father, like Stewart. The change was faster than it had any right to be. It was unnatural, certainly, and made her want to move away, but she was transfixed, unable to even turn her gaze as the magic took from him, devouring. Calum's guard rushed to his aid, but what would be left of him when the magic was done would be nothing at all of the man he'd been. Like Nim's father, Calum would be gone.

Nim swayed, caught by a pair of steadying arms before she crashed to the ground.

CHAPTER 27

Nim leaned into Maris, exhausted and blinking away her sense of unreality to find an entirely different scene than she'd expected. Margery stood beside her, hand on a dagger that she'd gotten from who knew where, Wes close at her side.

The higher-ranking Trust officials watched dispassionately, apparently not at all concerned at the state of their heir as he was dragged from the room.

"Where have you been?" Nim asked nonsensically as Maris helped her back to her feet.

"Thought it best that I assist Warrick from his bindings." Maris's voice was steady behind her, close, calm, and reassuring. It felt completely incongruous to the emotions still roaring through Nim.

Her eyes found Warrick, who stood with his mother. Nim and Warrick stared at each other for a long moment, the head of the Trust thrashing against bonds at her wrists and Rhen's hold on her arm. "What's happening?"

Nim's voice was feeble. An unwitting smile sneaked across Rhen's face as Warrick's voice rose through the chamber in answer. "My esteemed lady queen has saved the great kingdom of

Inara and, at grave peril, stood against what was unjust below. She has paid much in sacrifice, as has her father, her mother, and each of those who stand by her now in her moment of triumph. I bow to her, in deference, in loyalty, and in submission." His eyes met hers as he rose again. "Majesty, I am yours."

Nim blinked.

The head of the Trust shrieked.

Rhen tugged on his mother's bonds. "I see that it falls to me to deal with the most unpleasant of tasks, then." He addressed the crowd. "The head of the Trust has broken an ancient covenant with Inara by attacking its queen, by her own hands and with intent to kill." His gaze passed over those watching, but to Nim's eyes, none of the many, many Trust associates disagreed. "As such, and by the terms of that covenant, she will remain imprisoned to the end of her days, stripped of title, stripped of crown, bound from her connection to the source."

Warrick's mother shrieked again.

Margery's hand slipped into Nim's. Maris stood at her other shoulder, still providing support.

"It is with some regret that I must pass the title of King of Inara back to my brother, for now he is free and true heir, Stewart's firstborn son." A heartbeat passed in which something swelled between Rhen and Warrick, but it was gone before Nim could process exactly what it was. Rhen moved forward. "Furthermore, Calum, as eldest son and heir to the Trust, has become... incapable of rule. And with its previous head in irons, that title now falls to the next in line." He wet his lips. "Warrick has been tied by magic to his queen, Her Majesty Nimona Weston, and such a bond means that he is ineligible for Trust rule."

Nim gasped, but Warrick only remained, still and certain, entirely without remorse.

"So I, as last remaining heir, must take his place." Rhen handed the signet ring to Warrick, who slipped it onto his finger with no more than a brief nod of acknowledgment—as if the entire ordeal was not the great shock that was rocking through Nim.

Rhen sighed. "With that, I suppose I now crown myself head of the Trust."

There was a murmuring through the crowd—a crowd more massive than it had any right to be—that was more understanding and expectance than exuberant cheer. Margery let out a wobbly huff of breath. Nim looked at her friends. Wes was trembling, Maris serene, but each of them settling into their new reality with more composure than Nim. Her heart stuttered, her hands shaking.

They had done it. It had cost their families everything—Stewart and his advisors had given all and more—but they had won. Inara was no longer under siege. Wes, Allister, Margery's frivolous cousin, *everyone* was safe. Inara would stand.

A warm arm slid around Nim, drawing her from Maris's and Margery's support. She turned into Warrick's embrace, staring up at him in a bit of a daze as her arms wrapped around him of their own accord.

"My lady queen." His voice was low, eyes bright, so close that there might have been no one else in the world. "I have a great desire to repair to our suite." *Home*, his intimation said. Home in Inara Castle and in the arms of his wife. "Posthaste, if it please you."

The relief that washed over Nim had the edge of her lips tipping into a tenuous smile. "I can think of nothing that would please me more."

EPILOGUE

Margery stood on a balcony overlooking the grandest ballroom inside Inara Castle. Moonlight fell through the high windows, casting the stone in a silvery glow, but beneath, the crowd glided across a polished floor, wearing jewels and toasting with goblets that glinted in the flickering firelight.

It was a celebration. Inara's king and queen had returned and, with them, the safety of the kingdom. A few holdouts remained, some dissent among those at court, but any who knew, who truly understood what had happened between Stewart and the Trust and how close Inara had come to its downfall, had been nothing but grateful for how things had turned out.

Margery was one who understood. The Trust could not be brought under an Inaran king's control. A well of power ran beneath the kingdom, as fathomless and hungry as a great sea, and only one who held Trust blood could keep it under rein. The head of the Trust must be one of its own if Inara was to remain safe.

Margery's father had been taken by that power. Allister's charge—the gentleman Hearst—was gone as well. It had stolen so many of the kingdom's people, not just courtiers and those close to the king. They had found relief from the danger, finally and however temporarily, as long as its new head upheld his vow.

She sighed. "It's unbecoming to lurk in the shadows."

She did not have to look to see the grin crossing Rhen's lips —that smirk was practically burned into her memory. "You are a guest of honor. Are you not meant to be loitering among the highest of society?"

Rhen hummed as if considering, his saunter moving him near her spot at the rail. "I think, perhaps, that is precisely how I've found myself here."

Margery scoffed. The highest of society, she was not.

"You underestimate yourself, Lady Margery."

She'd been keeping her distance from Rhen—pointedly so— since he'd crowned himself head of the Trust. It had not been easy, given that Nim had raised Margery to royal advisor and had been forcing Rhen to attend as many functions as possible to drive home the point with the courtiers that the Trust was a true ally.

It had not been easy, but she'd managed. Every comment he made had been brushed aside, every attempt at goodwill taken with ill grace. Margery was nothing if not resolute. It might have worked if he'd been any other man. But he was not. Rhen could sense the truth, could feel precisely what Margery desired— whether he intended to or not.

"How did you know we would do it?" she asked. "How could you possibly be certain a couple of highborn society outsiders and a seneschal's messenger could pull this off?"

He huffed a laugh. "I did not. I am loath to admit it, but I had naught but the barest of hope."

Margery glanced at him sidelong. The glint in his eyes teased that there had been more than a bare hope. Margery knew that Warrick and Rhen had done all they might to help fate play out in their favor, in any case. He bit his lip as if hoping to keep her attention, but Margery forced herself to look away.

Rhen was quiet for a long while, simply standing beside her.

When he finally spoke, he did not move nearer, but his gentle voice somehow closed the distance even as his gaze remained with hers on the crowd below.

"I can feel your disquiet. Whatever secret you are afraid to surrender, however strongly you disdain it..." He swallowed. "I assure you, to someone like me, it is not a truth too terrible to overcome."

Something light and fluttery danced in Margery's stomach. She might have known he would realize—and not simply because of his ability to sense what she wanted. Rhen had seen her in the king's vault. He'd spent hours with her while she sat in stocking feet without asking why she'd abandoned fine shoes. And even if he'd not done those things, no one watched Margery as thoroughly as Rhen.

"I don't want your cures." Her voice was flat to her own ears, but nothing was to be done for it. Magic had gotten her there, and she would never bargain to undo it, particularly now that she understood the true cost. Margery took care of herself. She took care of her friends. She would never be so desperate again.

"You misunderstand, my lady. I would never presume to..." He breathed as if deliberating. "Well, I would presume, wouldn't I? I feel as if I am doing so right now. It was only that I meant to offer assurance—" He chuckled softly then shook his head. "I find that being candid is not my forte, if you'll beg pardon on the matter. I only meant to offer comfort. And should I not be able to appease you by a vow that I could not in the least be repelled by what hides beneath your secrets or whatever ill-gotten manner in which they came to be yours, then I would fall to my knees to offer what comfort might come from even the warmth of my touch."

Margery's insides went unsettlingly wrong-side up. She looked at him. His profile remained calm and open; he still faced the balcony rail as if to give her space. She would not tell him he was exceptionally good at candor. She would not admit how his words made her feel. "Your Highness, are you suggesting you would worship at my feet?"

"If that is where you wish me to start," he hedged.

There was no hiding her intake of breath. He turned to her, his eyes lit with an intensity that made her go soft. He apparently sensed the change in her. "May I touch you, Lady Margery?"

"Where?" was her reply, when clearly she meant *what*, and not at all as airy and ruffled as it had sounded.

"About your waist," he said, moving closer. "Very gently, so that you might not be tempted to flee upon my confession."

"Confession?"

He came closer still, the toes of his boots nearly brushing the tips of hers. "The confession that I would like very much to kiss you one day."

Margery swallowed, bringing herself, barely, under control. "Which day, precisely?"

He did not move closer, only watched her, studying her face as if he meant to memorize its form. "The first day which you allow it." His attention drifted up from her lips until their gazes locked, and his eyes glinted with mischief and magic. "And every day following that."

Thank you for reading the Between Ink and Shadows series!

Please read on for a preview of the new standalone epic fantasy
Beyond the Filigree Wall

*A dark curse. A deadly secret. The ill-fated girl at the heart
of both.*

BEYOND THE FILIGREE WALL

PREVIEW

The good king-fearing people of Westrende held a single faith without question: *magic isn't real*. Stories of fae were only constructs designed to explain away the sort of unpleasantness no one wished to examine overmuch—unpleasantness like the madness that struck when the moon was full, when a maiden went lost, a child fell ill, or perhaps when a king's gold was stolen and the wheat stores turned foul. That sort.

Myth, superstition, and deception were what the tales were made of.

Etta, neither unreservedly good nor especially king-fearing, knew the truth was far simpler. Beneath their willful ignorance and outright denial rested a dark secret, depthless in its desire for vengeance. Indeed, the people of the kingdom had no notion that they were only a single misstep from plummeting over a deadly precipice. They liked it that way.

Lady Antonetta Ostwind, sole daughter and heir of the great General Ostwind, had kept that vile secret since she was a girl. *Tell no one*, her father had warned in whispered threats. Tell no one of the monsters who'd come for her mother while Etta had watched from the darkness beneath her bed. *Speak of them, and they shall come again.* She had bitten down on the words until she tasted blood. She had not spoken, had not screamed, had not uttered a single word of the fae in all the days which followed.

It had not stopped their coming because the fae had been there all along.

Antonetta could see through their glamour. Her father's fear and the king's council may have kept Etta from shouting the truth, but it could not take her sight. The fae, magical beings intent on doing harm, walked among them. Lesser fae may have seemed harmless if not for the shadows—beings like those who had taken her mother, darker in both intent and form. Shadows, they were called, because to acknowledge the existence of the high fae of the Riven Court was to meet a disagreeable fate.

Etta had been forced into a secrecy meant to protect her, but it had protected only the monsters. She understood precisely the ruin they caused because she could see a truth at which no one else dared look. The fae were worse than any imagined tales. And her silence had kept them safe. Her hands had not spilled their blood.

All that was about to change.

❧

"Nearly there," Nickolas chirped. Blond, approaching five and twenty, and apparently entirely at ease being cramped inside a juddering cabin for days, Nickolas Brigham—Etta's escort, onetime childhood friend, and several-time nemesis—had been unashamedly vying for her attention for the entire trip.

Etta stared out the window of the carriage. There was nothing particularly outstanding beyond the cloudy glass, but there was equally nothing outstanding about her, and she wasn't fool enough to believe his attentions were genuine. Nickolas was tall and handsome and had the sort of crooked smile that made many a knee go weak. Though passable in many respects, Etta was little different than the other ladies at court, of which he surely had his pick. She understood full well that his attention—

like nearly all attentions she'd been paid since she was young—came not from any special beauty or grace but from her standing.

As head of the council, Etta's father was the most influential of a dozen men and women who directed the fate of the kingdom and all those within it until a king was returned to power—which, at the rate things were going, would not be anytime soon. It was no secret that the current prospects were all a good decade short of meeting the age and education requirements to become king, and two of those prospects had recently been stricken ill.

Furthermore, in a matter of days, Etta herself would become marshal, head of law and order in the kingdom and responsible for overseeing the guard. She was not about to cock it up for a boy like Nickolas, who would get no further than captain without an advantageous marriage. She drew in a long breath, comforted by what was to come once she was finally installed into the office of marshal. The position was significant in that it alone allowed freedom of movement beyond the council. She'd be tied no longer to their foolish rules and society games. They would be unable to stop her from crossing the Rive.

"You must be excited to return after all these years," Nickolas said. "Eager? Relishing the tingle of anticipatory glee, perhaps?"

She continued her regard of the unkempt grass beyond the carriage window. The seemingly endless expanse of sky had been overcast most of the day and was beginning to color with a tinge of pink to herald the coming sunset. The trip had been planned in exacting detail to allow for the carriage's timely arrival—even if that arrival was two days prior to her father's expectations—because none were allowed to cross the border once night had fallen.

The kingdom gates, twisted dark iron topped with deadly barbs, tucked neatly between walls of the finest stone, came into view. A line of kingsmen stared down from the parapets, surely aware even from such a height who warranted the pomp of the approaching caravan. She would be scrutinized regardless. They would make her wait outside the gates while her documents were verified, even with Nickolas and his ilk at her side. She glanced back to the rest of her escort, kingsmen of varying status perched in full regalia atop prized horses. More than one of her protectors seemed to have an eye on the line of trees in the distance. Even Nickolas seemed a bit fidgety in the dying light.

It was telling that the people of Westrende denied the existence of fae and magic, yet not a soul seemed comfortable with a wait outside the gates so near where the dark forest loomed. As if the Rive might reach out and snatch them.

Etta scoffed. "Nickolas," she said, finally giving him her gaze. "Tell me what I have missed."

His smile was golden, a great, glowing, ridiculous thing that seemed to light up the carriage. By the wall, he had always been so mulishly oblivious. She wasn't certain he'd ever been able to read a person's mood—or maybe he'd simply not bothered to care if, in the end, doing so didn't further his cause. One more trait it seemed he'd not outgrown. She gestured for him to get on with it.

"Little has happened that was not relayed in your reports, I'm sure, my lady." His smile hinted that he in fact knew exactly what she was about—mood and all—and intended to toy with her.

She gave him her flattest expression.

His grin shifted into something a bit more tenable. "Lady Yates is having a torrid affair with a barber's son. Theo's carpenter was caught using funds meant for suite furnishings to procure an absolutely obscene collection of crystal urns, which were discovered by a maid while freshening the mattresses." He waved a hand vaguely near the curtain, as if drawing the memories from air. "A pair of scribes was caught desecrating the king's garderobe, and the magistrate had them pilloried in their smallclothes for a week."

She managed not to wince. Castle gossip wasn't at all something she'd missed about being away, and certainly not the information she'd been after from Nickolas. "What of the new chancellor?"

The answering spark in his eyes teased something that Etta did not like at all. He leaned forward on the seat, his long fingers woven together only inches from her knee, the scent of roses and sandalwood wafting off him. "Ah, yes," he said. "Gideon."

Gideon. He was going to be hideous. She could tell already. "Yes."

"Nephew to our great steward."

Etta had never met the new chancellor but had heard well enough: he was a brutal tactician with no regard for new ideas, no interest in improvement to their ancient laws and inter-kingdom protocol, and not a whit of tolerance for those who crossed the wall. "He's a traditionalist," she said.

Nickolas chuckled. "You could say that."

"I did. What would *you* say?"

He leaned back, tossing his hands a bit before sliding them over the slick blue fabric that covered his knees. "I'd call him a raging cumberground. An absolute saddle-goose. Ineffective as a boat full of holes." He shrugged. "But that's just me."

Well, now he was just trying to buy her with flattery. Etta nodded. "We shall see."

The man had been installed after she'd gone away—been sent away—for her training. In the nearly four years since, he'd risen to the head of chancery with unlikely speed. It was a position that rivaled hers. There was every expectation he would become the marshal's mortal enemy.

Etta intended to crush him.

⚜

After they had been permitted through the gates and winded their way through the kingdom under a sky that had turned turbulent, the carriage, at long last, drew to a stop before their

179

destination. Said destination was not the front entrance of the castle to a grand reception, as would surely have been planned by her father's staff. Etta had demanded that Nickolas both keep their arrival confidential and deliver her to the service entrance. She needed to prepare for her reintroduction to the council and courtiers on her own terms, and in time to suss out what else they might have planned for her. Besides, she wanted greatly to wash the days of travel from her person before meeting a single soul.

Shoving a lock of her chestnut hair behind an ear and sorting her disheveled skirt into order, she drew a fortifying breath of stuffy cabin air.

When she glanced up, Nickolas was watching her, a sly grin on his stupid charming mouth. "Ready, my lady?"

She would not reward him with a glare, never mind that his tone had been loaded. They both knew she was walking blindly into a lion's den, against the general's orders. "Nickolas," she said, "I am always—"

His bark of laughter broke the stillness she only then realized had come over them. He placed a hand over his heart and slid forward in his seat. "Yes, it is not as if you have ever let me forget." The door opened, and his long legs carried him past her in one graceful motion to land outside the carriage and between a waiting pair of umbrella-wielding ushers. He leaned in and adopted a conspiratorial tone. "The lady Ostwind is always ready."

Despite the dread that sank in her belly, Etta took his proffered hand. "Yes," she said. "Always."

Etta was not ready. A single flash of her reflection in the ornate metal trim that lined the carriage door made her state painfully clear. She stepped out regardless, just as the murky sky let loose and poured rain onto the fine cobbled drive.

Nickolas glanced at the deluge, taking hold of one umbrella while leaving the second for the ushers. "Portentous."

She resisted the urge to jab an elbow into his ribs. The space between the carriage and the entrance was excessive and scattered with mounted kingsmen eager to return their charge. Until the general's daughter was safely inside, their duty was not complete. Etta took hold of the umbrella with Nickolas, and they weaved swiftly between the beasts with their clattering hooves and the castle staff converging on the carriage to retrieve the pair's many trunks.

Beneath the overhang at the entrance, Etta stopped to shake the umbrella and draw another breath. Her apprehension was nearly under control when a black dog shot from beyond a column to dart past her skirts. She shrieked—an absolute embarrassment she would dwell on when she wasn't thusly occupied—leaping back into Nickolas, who brushed off the arms of his embroidered suitcoat.

Clearly not expecting the collision, he barely caught her before they both tumbled to sprawl on the rain-soaked cobblestone. As it was, his boot splashed into an impossibly fast-forming puddle, splattering wet filth up the leg of his fine trousers and half of Etta's skirt. She did not bother with explanation or apology because in that moment, she became aware that the creature had been no dog at all.

It had been a lesser fae. Etta said a curse, gritted her teeth, and took tighter hold of the closed umbrella. Stomping through the door on its trail, she dodged two serving men and a downstairs maid before she caught sight of the dark mass of fur sliding around a corner. She was after it without another thought.

Etta had made a promise to herself while she'd been away: not a single fae would pass her sight without coming to regret it. Her silence was over. They would pay for what they had done.

The thing darted into a storeroom, turning to give her a savage grin made of too many teeth before the door slammed closed behind it. Etta picked up her pace, shoving through after it, rain-soaked weapon in hand. The door snicked shut behind her, throwing the narrow room into near darkness. The creature had disappeared, but she could feel its eyes upon her and almost sense the horrid glee vibrating through it.

A drop of rain fell from her umbrella to splat loudly on the pantry floor. In the shadows, something giggled.

"Come out, you filthy—"

A solid slab of wood smacked into Etta from behind, Nickolas and the light of the main room coming along with it. The creature shot across the space, and Etta took an off-balance swing just as Nickolas grabbed her in some dramatic and entirely misplaced heroic gesture that she made a note to discuss with him at a later date. The swing missed, the umbrella thwacked into a sack of flour, and Etta was quite suddenly covered in a matted, pale paste. The creature shoved her to land face-first into the sack then darted out the open door.

Etta lay there for a moment, swallowing words she'd sworn she would never eat again. A lock of hair was wedged into her mouth. Her knee throbbed. And the beast must have gotten a swipe in on its way through because she felt the thin stinging line of the cuts she'd grown accustomed to as a girl. Several cuts, it seemed, began to burn near her ankle.

"By the wall," Nickolas murmured, staring down at the mess in apparent awe.

"The wall indeed," she said through gritted teeth then flopped to her back so she could glare up at him.

They came out of the storeroom to an audience of at least a dozen kingsmen and castle staff. Etta slapped a hand to her skirt, which puffed what flour had not yet caked on, then threw the umbrella to the floor. "Ladies, gentlemen, so good to see you once more." Then she tottered off on flour-caked heels without a single look back.

Nickolas found her in the first empty corridor she'd come to, pounding her fists on the wall with a curse entirely unseemly for one of her station.

"Etta," he said, his voice low, careful, and not at all in a tone he'd used in their many days of travel.

"No. Don't. Just—I need to return to my rooms."

"Absolutely," he answered with not a single question about why she had just attempted murder on a rangy dog. "Only"—he glanced over his shoulder—"let me be certain word of this doesn't leave the, uh…"

Etta groaned.

"Right," he said. "One moment."

She turned to lean against the wall of the empty corridor, jerked her wet gloves off, and threw them to the floor. The narrow passage was used by staff, poorly lit, sparsely decorated, and unlikely to be occupied at the current hour. Not that it mattered. She'd been planning her triumphant return to Westrende since the day she was shipped off to school. And there she was, all her care and caution exhausted within minutes of her arrival.

She unbuttoned her lace-trimmed jacket and yanked her arms free of the damp material, tearing seams by the sound of it. It went in a pile with her gloves. Bending over to ruck up her skirts, she cursed again when she saw the damage the thing had done to her leg. "This is why I hate dogs," she muttered, as if in reply to all the remembered comments she'd been unable to answer to honestly since she was a girl. "Cannot trust a single one not to be fae."

She snapped the skirt down and wrapped her arms around her middle, wondering if she might succeed in navigating to her rooms without Nickolas there to clear a path. By the sight of her, it was probably best she didn't try. She sighed, closed her eyes, and leaned back against the wood-paneled wall.

Door, her mind corrected just as it fell open behind her. She fell with it. Her arms went out, scrabbling for purchase, and caught only one side of the frame. She felt more than heard the intake of breath of the person she'd pitched into and drew herself up to turn and look. It was a dark-haired man in his early twenties, impossibly near. His square jaw had gone slack in an improbably perfect face, everything else about him entirely buttoned up. He wore a high-collared black shirt beneath a well-fitted black suit, not a lick of fanciful trim upon him. Against his chest was clutched a sleeve of parchment, his long fingers curling more possessively around it as she watched.

Then her eyes rose to his, dark beneath thick lashes and soft with something akin to bewilderment. That was when she remembered, quite suddenly, that half her clothes were strewn across the floor.

"Oh," she said, searching for anything at all she might say to the poor man. She drew herself up. "Lord—" She stopped and cleared her throat, unsure of his identity. He seemed vaguely familiar, but she had been gone for four years. People changed.

"Lord Alex—" he started almost automatically then abruptly cut himself off to stare back at her. He did not appear to have the same sort of trouble with recognition Etta was experiencing. His tone changed. "What precisely are you about?"

Her mouth came open without a single answer in mind just as Nickolas burst back into the hallway, announcing, "Done, we're covered. Saved you from a spanking no doubt—" His words fell off, his wink and stride stuttering to an awkward halt as he took in the scene.

He decidedly did not look down at Etta's clothes on the floor or her person, which gained him a point in her tally, but neither did he explain what they were about, which, to be fair, seemed unlikely to be believable in any case. He cleared his throat, not unlike what Etta had just done.

The new arrival glanced between them, apparently making his own assumptions. "This behavior is entirely unseemly for persons of your station."

Nickolas ran a hand over his chest, seeming to fight a smile. "Quite." He stepped forward, resuming his casual posture as he approached the pair. He held an arm toward Etta. "My lady. Perhaps we shall take this kind advice in the spirit it was given and remove ourselves to your rooms."

Etta's gaze darted between Nickolas and the other man. She

felt her cheeks heat, but she was not sure precisely where to direct her ire, had she even the energy to unleash it. She decided she didn't have to. She was an Ostwind. Without a word in farewell, she bent to pick up her things then turned and strode away, Nickolas's chuckle echoing behind her.

Thank you for reading this sample preview of *Beyond the Filigree Wall*. Find it at www.melissa-wright.com or your favorite retailer.

SHATTERED REALMS

King of Ash and Bone

Queen of Iron and Blood

- WITCHY PNR -

HAVENWOOD FALLS

Toil and Trouble

BAD MEDICINE

Blood & Brute & Ginger Root

Visit the author on the web at

www.melissa-wright.com

9 781950 958535